My Name is Kozha

Berdibek Sokpakbaev

Metropolitan Classics

The book "My Name is Kozha" , written by the noted Kazakh writer Berdibek Sokpakbaev, is the second book of the series of books of classic Kazakh writers published English, which the Kazakh PEN-club decided to publish in the USA. The book collection "We Are Kazakhs" is being published under the supervision of the President of Kazakh PEN-club

Mr. BIGELDY GABDULLIN

MY NAME IS KOZHA

Berdibek Sokpakbayev

Translated from Russian by
Catherine A. Fitzpatrick

Metropolitan Classics

ISBN: 978-1-57480-002-9

PRINTED IN THE UNITED STATES OF AMERICA

ACKNOWLEDGEMENTS

The Publishers would like to express their gratitude to the Kazakh PEN-club for their constant support and attention to this project. Initially, it was but an ambitious idea of the Kazakh PEN-club President, **Mr. Gabdullin**, to allow for the best works of Kazakh classic writers be known globally, by way of their translation into English. Step by step, due to the tireless efforts of **Mr. Gabdullin**, the project received the financial and logistical support from influential Kazakh state organizations and private companies.

The translation of this book was possible due to the generous support of the "KazMunayGaz" company. We also would like to thank the Ambassador of Kazakhstan in the USA and the Representative of Kazakhstan in the United Nations, for their vital support of this project.

FOREWORD

As a brief forward to Berbidek Sokpkbaev's "My name is Kozha", I would like to convey certain details about my father, regarding not only his nature as a person, but also as a writer. Perhaps this might add a splash of color to this novel, which has been deemed a gem of Kazakh literature, and has also received much acclaim far beyond the country's borders.

My father was born in 1924 in a tiny, rural Kazakh village. His family lived in total poverty, and at the tender age of eight, he suffered the loss of his mother. The pain of her passing was a wound that his soul was never fully able to heal. His great love for learning was instilled in him by his older brother, whose life was cut short by the Great Patriotic War. My father, at a very early age, was forced to overcome great hardships, endured starvation, all while lacking any maternal care or comfort. Nevertheless, he was a cheerful and curious child, who very much enjoyed burrowing his face in books. His penchant for learning eventually drew the young man to the capital, where he applied to the university, and was accepted into the Philological Department, which he graduated with flying colors. It was there that he met his future wife, my mother.

Raised in an environment tainted by constant lack in rural Kazakh villages, far removed from the city way of life, my parents were able to transform themselves into learned, cultured, well-read and spiritual individuals. Our home was always unadorned and modest, we had only the barest of necessities. In spite of this, we had a wonderful library – the one investment on which our resources were never spared. I distinctly remember my father once said, half-joking, that pocketing anything is, of course, not honorable ⌐ hold for one exception – books. He believed that if for some reason, one is refused in an attempt to obtain a book, such an act should not be deemed shameful. My parents often frequented the theatre, museums and galleries both in Alma-Aty and even more so in Moscow, where we resided while my father completed his graduate literary studies. Their familiarity with the realm of all things beautiful, and their insatiable thirst for spiritual enrichment were an integral facet of our family life. My father was a handsome and charming gentleman, who possessed a sharp mind, wit and a splendid sense of humor. It is no coincidence that authors such as Bernard Shaw and Mark Twain made his list of favorites. Plots for his stories, both long and short, were often taken from experiences in his own life. For example, when I was five – and my parents, on their way to work would leave me alone in the house, they would always lock the door with a large, hanging padlock. Being left alone locked up, for hours on end was not something I was fond of, so one particular evening I had decided to hide the loathsome object in the stove. Not surprisingly, they were unable to locate it and thus, for a brief time, I had obtained my long-awaited freedom. Finally, there came a day when my deception was uncovered. My father, admiring my ingenuity, was awfully amused, and this incident proved to be the inspiration for one of his own humorous stories, which he aptly titled – "Padlock".

My father's boundless talent, paired with his richness of life experiences prompted an avid and early start in his creative literary endeavors. His writing spanned multiple genres, and he wrote for both young and old. Each book he churned out – whether poetry or prose, thanks to his colorful and unique style, instantly gained popularity, bringing the young author well-deserved acclaim. His stories were eagerly published throughout Kazakhstan, without restriction, until, that is – they began to depict pain. His first few major stories and novels, significant both in their form and context, displayed his matured writing style which illustrated, in an, oftentimes, brutally honest fashion, the reality of that era, and were further inspired by his interactions with those who surrounded him. Candid, his writing retained a certain purity – no frills, embellishment or deceit. One of his first major works - "My Name is Kozha", was immediately met with hostility by the authorities, and a ban was issued on its publication. Unyielding, officials staunchly opposed the unabashedly transparent portrayal of the reality of the life and people in rural Kazakh villages.

Luckily, my father would not be discouraged, and decided to appear with the manuscript at a conference for young writers in Moscow, to which he had been invited as a participant. It was there, that this noteworthy novel was praised, attracting the attention of the Russian literary circle. His distinct and colorful style also deeply impacted the renowned French author Louis Aragon, who personally arranged for the novel to be translated and published in France. Only then was the novel finally approved to be released in Kazakhstan, and to this day remains one of the proud crowning jewels of Kazakh literature.

This had been the first notorious, strained success of the young Kazakh author. Unfortunately, this would not be his last bout with opposition. His next novel would await a similarly tense and challenging fate on its way to the masses. You see, my father was not known for his flattery. He was not one to appease and persuade the officials, nor was he capable of bending to their whim – in fact, he possessed a great disdain for them. The unremitting censorship, changes and editing demanded of him in order for his creations to see the light of day left him feeling beaten. The novel "My Name is Kozha" was soon turned into a film of the same name, and subsequently won one of the top prizes at the Cannes Film Festival. To this day, it remains the only Kazakh children's movie, and has received considerable acclaim, internationally. The author's popularity continued to grow, and he became known across the USSR, and then – globally. He amassed a considerable income. But, his heart was wounded, his pain – incurable. He felt robbed of his ability to write authentically, as he truly desired. Forced to bend to the will of the officials political agenda (which would ultimately leave his work a mangled remnant of what it had once been) made living and certainly creating an intolerable endeavor. To make matters worse, the author's personal life suffered great discord as well, which would ultimately lead to the collapse of his family.

The thorny, complex creative fate, the inability of his soul to attain any semblance of peace or satisfy his true ambitions as a writer, stripped the author, leaving a deep sense of helplessness that would give birth to his addiction to alcohol. My father underwent treatment at several rehabilitation facilities, yet each time the effect was short-lived. He became withdrawn, ill-tempered and grew ever the more disenchanted with life. The Writer's Union and the country house on the outskirts of town were the only two places he was able to find real solace. In the Writer's Union he was given a private office, and the post of literary consultant. The Union sheltered the author, providing the immersive creative environment he so desperately needed, and offered him the ability to interact with like-minded writers. In the quiet solitude of his country home, the author spent most of his time reading or writing, though in his final years, he seemed to lose all hope in publishing the fruits of his creative labors.

My father made no attempt to conceal his highly critical views of the soviet reality, and voiced his opinions often among his circle of writers and friends. This information, of course, made its way up the ladder to the officials, further exacerbating the author's already delicate position. He was straightforward and prone to speaking his mind, thereby guaranteeing himself a list of enemies. Oftentimes, he would put down a newspaper or turn off the radio or television, and exclaim: "Lies! All of it – lies!" Over the years, I would come to realize that he perceived and comprehended the reality on a far broader and deeper spectrum than most, a trait that is inherent only in certain outstanding individuals, who are wise and astute.

"My Name is Kozha" can easily be classified as an autobiographical work, for the majority of characters and events that occurred within the story were real, and the prototype for the main character was without a doubt Berbidek Sokpakbaev himself. This wonderful work has gained praise internationally, and readers have been falling in love with it from the very beginning. To this day, it is one of the most beloved books of many a generation of Kazakh readers. The reason for the immense popularity and success of this book is simple – the history, portrayed within the novel, is honest – each one of us can identify with it, relate to it. Everyone who has read it, has been able to recognize some part of themselves – be it their childhood or their experiences in school. Of course, these years have receded into the past, for children are growing up in a much different world now – yet, the vibrant and memorable character, the young rascal, distinguished by his honesty, bravery, warmth and mischievousness is able to, even now, rouse our keenest interest and our deepest sympathies. Each and every one of us. The story is clever, kind-heartedly ironic and deeply human and it is in this regard that it is reminiscent of the widely known works by Mark Twain - "The Adventures of Tom Sawyer" and "The Adventures of Huckleberry Finn".

Some years ago, it became my professional responsibility to begin translating fine Kazakh literature into the Russian language. My father suddenly and with great surprise discovered my abrupt transition in careers paths (I had graduated with a degree in chemistry, and was currently advancing in that field). It seems he had been keeping tabs on my more creative endeavors, perhaps with the aid of his literary circle, because one day, out of the blue, he approached me with an offer to translate one of his best works – "My Name is Kozha". This was, indeed, a great undertaking and I hope that I have made him proud. Sadly, it is not fated for him to know of its publication in America, but I am incredibly proud and thankful to have been able to, in the very least, contribute by laying down the foundation for its translation. I would like to use this opportunity to express my deepest thanks to all for whom this book is designated by birth.

Having earned his nation's affection and devotion whilst still alive, having glorified alongside other major Kazakh writers our nation's literature far beyond the borders of our motherland, all the while remaining the undisputed master of artistic prose, B. Sokpakbaev has not once received any award or recognition for his literature. I am certain, if my father were to know that his work is being published to this very day, that his books are not collecting dust on bookstore shelves and that screenings of the film are still packing theatres – he would be ever so pleased. To have such recognition of the whole nation is certainly a great success!

In conclusion, I would like to express my hope that this simple, yet dynamic, human and poignant tale of one Kazakh youth, may resonate with the hearts of many new readers, for honesty, kindness, love and righteousness – no matter who we are, or from where we hail, these are the timeless treasures inherent in all of us!

Samal Sokpakbaeva. Almaty. July, 2015.

TABLE OF CONTENTS

PREFACE

Allahu![1] I am not bragging my friends, I am telling you the pure truth: my dream of becoming a writer no matter what was born in me from my childhood years. Already in third or fourth grade, my fame as a poet had crossed the threshold of the school and flew around the aul[2]. People even began to call me "the boy poet."

At first, this nickname pricked me like a pricker. But then I decided: talent is inherent in a person at birth. I didn't ask anyone for my talent and I did not steal it. And if that's how it was, if I am given this by fate, then nothing else remains to do but make peace with it.

They say that major poets write their verses only when inspiration falls upon them. As for me, it's as if inspiration was always hanging at the tip of my pen. I have only to find a minute and sit down at the desk when I will immediately compose something. What am I saying! Sometimes it happens that I will begin a new notebook of verse and I want to fill it up so fast that I give myself a task: to compose each day a certain number of poems.

A person grows by nature, and I was no exception. Day after day, I grew more and more visibly. Soon my poems began to be regularly published in the class and school wall newspapers[3]. It even got to the point where I didn't offer my poems; I was asked to think up something appropriate.

"Write some poetry about May!" some people asked.

"How many couplets do you need?"

"Four is enough."

"Alright," I replied and immediately, right at the lesson, I fulfilled my promise.

"Compose something about discipline!" asked others.

"What would it cost you to dash off a verse about those who sleep during lessons? Only first, praise someone from among the kids who set an example, and then criticize, or else it turns out from start to finish to be nothing but criticism."

These and other orders were showered on me like snow from the unit and class editorial boards.

All of this brought me at first enormous joy, but in time in turned into a routine task and ceased to inspire me. The more often my verse appeared on the wall newspapers, the less they attracted my attention and concerned me.

---

[1] *Allahu Akhbar* is the Arabic phrase for "God is Great," said by Muslims.

[2] An aul is a village in Central Asia, where usually people live in yurts or cabins and pasture their animals nearby.

[3] Wall newspapers were common in the Soviet Union, originally due to shortage of newsprint after the 1917 revolution. They were a means of Communist Party education of workers and students, and sometimes their participation was enlisted in the form of articles, photography, poetry and artwork.

In my opinion, a person is led ahead only by a dream. And now I dreamed that my poems would be set in typographic fonts and published by a real publishing house so that people bought them and read them. Oh, how wonderful that would be! Fresh issues of Pioner [Pioneer] would be brought to our school and they would began to hand them out to the kids. Someone who was the first to open the magazine would exclaim, "Hey, look! Our Kozha's poetry has been published here!" And my poem really would be there, and clearly, like a brand on the flank of a stallion, would be the name "Kozha Kadyrov."

Oh, if only that had really happened, what would Zhanar have thought about me? Likely she would have believed in my talent, that someday, I would become a famous writer. Then perhaps, she would treat me a little differently.

And what would that nasty Zhantas start doing, I wonder? He would probably burst from envy! Although no, most likely he would not get flustered and would say that probably somebody else with the name Kozha Kadyrov had written that. That is very much what you could expect from him.

I began leafing through all my poems, picking out what seemed to be the best ones to me, and hoping for success, sent them to Almaty, to the editorial board of the journal Pioner. Thus began my "bombing" of the capital with my poems.

I don't know what the reason was but not a single one of them, strange as it sounds, was published in the magazine. So then I tried a trick. I re-wrote the poems that had been sent to Pioner and sent them to the newspaper Kazakhstan Pioneri. Maybe they would like them there? But nothing came of that project. That newspaper evidently didn't find my works to their taste, either.

Despite these failures, I did not get dejected. In fact, my stubbornness grew. I took the trouble to re-write some of my most successful poems and sent them around in several copies to all the publishing houses and editorial boards I knew. You would think that if a publisher didn't get my mailing, he would be offended. Of course, I was counting on the fact that if one publisher didn't print me, others would. From my fervor, I didn't realize that I had sent a letter with a collection of verses even to the editorial board of the journal Bloknot Agitatora [Agitator's Notebook]. And when I got a reply from there, I was ready to sink through the floor from embarrassment. The editors humorously replied that a person who did not understand what he was writing for could not become a good writer.

The only thing that nevertheless made me happy were the replies that came back from all the places where I had sent my verses. "It must be noted that you possess a certain poetic talent; however, it is necessary to work hard, to refine your craft and read as much as possible," is what they usually wrote me, or approximately what they wrote. Yet these brief encouraging lines inspired me and gave me strength. I proudly showed my friends the envelopes with the publishing houses' seals. Let them know who they are dealing with!

But some letters were prickly and pitiless. I remember one famous poet once wrote me: "I think that it's too early to stuff your head with poetry. I don't find anything interesting and personal in your verses." These words for me were like a rock suddenly falling on my head. Naturally, I hid such harsh and unpleasant replies immediately from outside eyes and destroyed them before they would destroy my fame as a school poet.

In the end, I grew disappointed in each of the editorial boards. Imagine how much money I spent on buying envelopes and stamps for sending letters! And all for nothing! I would have done better to buy a bunch of candies and enjoy them to the full.

Well, let it go! They didn't want to print it – and they don't have to! Even so, no matter what happens, I have not taken a single step from my sworn dream. Here, as you see, to spite them all, I have left poetry for awhile and have taken to writing this tale here. And so that everything will be as in a book, I have divided the events into chapters and have given each one a title. I promise you that I will not make up anything.

CHAPTER ONE

In Which the Reader Meets the Main Character, or To Be More Precise, Me

My name is…

When I try to pronounce my name, it's like my tongue sticks to the roof of my mouth. It seems to me that a pretty name is a real good fortune for a person. Take, for example, names like Murat, Bolat, Erbol, Bakhyt. They are easy to pronounce and pleasant to the ear. Moreover, as our Kazakh language teacher says, Maykanova-*tate*[4], they have a high ideological meaning. I note that those who have successful names are proud of it and loudly give their name when you make their acquaintance.

But you sometimes encounter names which are not only hard to pronounce but are also hard to listen to. And if you have that kind of name, then it's not even a question of other people, you yourself are the first not to like it. Of course, if you had the power, you would immediately change your name and would take for yourself something prettier. Alas! In that long-ago time when you were a tiny, rosy baby and lay in a cradle, your relatives, and maybe someone from among the respected guests, having fun at a *shildekhan*[5] and taking advantage of your helplessness, up and condemned you to one of the stupidest and most ridiculous names you could find on earth. Okembay's son, for example, was named *Tynzhyrtar*.[6] They say that at the *shildekhan*, one of the celebrating guests shouted his name with laughter, making an approving noise, and supported him as if to say, "you couldn't think up something better," and let the parents call their child such a name.

Thus, from the moment of birth, the name given to a baby sticks to him, as if it appeared on the earth with him. And you can never get away from it. No matter how repugnant it is to you, it is connected to you now to the end of your days.

---

[4] Address for an older person.
[5] A shildekhan is a celebration on the occasion of the birth of a baby.
[6] Literally, "exploding virgin land."

What can you say, there are quite a few injustices in life like this. Once I read in the newspaper how the Chinese give names to their children. The article really interested me. It turns out that in China, children do not have names until the ages of five or six, and in their families, they are called variously, "middle one," "little one," "beloved," sweetie," and so on. When the child turns five or six, he himself picks his own name as he wishes. Now there's fairness! Don't you think?

Well, alright. As they say, it's a matter of the past, like it or not – you can't fix it now. So let me get right down to business. So, my name is Kozha. As you can see, there's nothing remarkable about my name. Although, to be precise, originally I was not called Kozha, but Kozhabergen. Yes, yes, that's how it's written on my birth certificate. But what turns life doesn't take on the earth! In time, the tail of "Kozhabergen" fell off and disappeared without a trace. When this amazing turn occurred is not known. No one can name the year, month or day when this happened.

In general, as long as I can remember myself, I've been Kozha. Everybody who knows me in our parts calls me that.

We have two Kozhas in our class. The eldest son of Suttebay, is also named Kozha just like me. In order not to mix us up and know which one they mean, the guys gave us nicknames – I'm called Black Kozha and he's called White Kozha, evidently in accordance with how we look.[7]

At first I was mad at my nickname, but then gradually I got used to it and answer to it now without any offense. But some loud-mouths, like our Zhantas, didn't find this enough. Deliberately fracturing an already unpleasant nickname, they would tease me now and then with "Hey, Black Kozhe[8]!" Sometimes out of habit I would immediately answer, but later…boy, did those bullies get it!

My last name is Kadyrov. At one time, I wrote: Kadyruly.[9] But when I noticed that everybody else's last name ended in "ov," I decided not to stand out and became Kadyrov.

Kadyr is my father. Now what a complicated thing is life! At the word "father," my heart is ready to burst. How close and dear that word is to me. My friends quite often brag to each other – one guy's father bought him something, another's father bought him something. Yet another's father crafted something, or another's told him something. But I don't even know what kind of person my father was. I was two years old when he left for the front. What can a silly little two-year-old understand and remember? I never saw my father again after that. He never returned from the war…

My poor father! Who knows, if he were alive now – perhaps I'd be a little different. Perhaps I became the famous prankster Kozha precisely because I grew up without a father…

---

[7] The Russian word for skin is *kozha*.

[8] *Kozhe* means millet soup. Millet is a black grain.

[9] Dadyruly – "son of Kadyr" a variety of Kazakh last name.

But whatever you say, everybody needs a father. Even shaky decrepit oldsters sometimes sigh and remember their fathers.

And does a man need a woman? I think very much. Sometimes when my mother sits down at the table and goes through the photographs of my father, gazing at each one for a long time, I see tears on her eyelashes, and such a hopeless sorrow on her face that I feel unbearably sorry for her. But is that only from my pity? I understand why she is sad.

If her husband, and my father, were still alive, the shameless Karatay wouldn't be able to bother her, much less dare to sit near her.

Now, so to say, you've become acquainted with me. But in a work of art, after all, you have to not just say something about the hero, what he is like, but describe his face, the way he looks. So I guess I'll have to do that. But wait just a minute. I'll look at myself in the mirror first... So, there's my nose. My grandmother often says I'm pug-nosed. And she's absolutely right about that.

My nostrils, each of which I can freely stick a finger into, yawn open like the ends of a double-barreled pistol, and I have a round and completely shaven head. My hair has been completely removed with a razor by the old man, Aubakir, and my head looks a lot like a watermelon.

Oh, my hair! It's just as coarse and prickly as a pig's bristles. In our entire aul, there is only one person who has a razor that can handle it. That's Aubakir's razor. But even his razor at first would trip and snag in my bushy hair. Each time he would take up his razor, Aubakir would shake his head in surprise as if he were seeing me for the first time.

"*Yapyray*[10]! To be born with such hair! It isn't hair but some kind of prickers! Real prickers! You can see your mischievous character in this hair."

So, what else haven't I told you? I already mentioned my dark skin at the very beginning. And under my left ear, I have a little birth mark. What a stupid place it found! If it had settled somewhere on my face, let's say on my cheek, I think it would be much more beautiful. Last year, one of my teeth…although is it worth talking about it? Who doesn't have bad teeth? Besides, its absence is almost not noticeable.

Some people claim that I am not very tall, but my grandmother is just the opposite. She always says that I'm like my father – he was well-built and tall. Only God knows which of them is right. Last fall, when the school doctor measured our height, I was 130 centimeters tall. If Aubakir had not shaved my head, it would be 140 (undoubtedly, this is one of the down sides of a shaved head). I've already turned 12, and soon I will finish fifth grade.

With this, I will finish the first chapter of my tale and go on to the next.

---

[10] *Yapyray* is an expression of surprise in the Kazakh language.

CHAPTER TWO

In Which We Will Talk About Karatay

Running around playing soccer all day, at the end of the day I was completely tuckered out. During the game, when you're seized with enthusiasm, you don't notice how tired you are. And now I was going home, barely dragging my weakened legs, covered with a thick layer of dust. "Oh, I wish I could jump in the water now!" I thought and threw a glance at the creek which ran nearby. Some girls were happily splashing there. Let them swim, they're probably hot, too. But I'll first have something to eat, or else my stomach is growling so much that I think I could swallow a whole camel with its entire load.

Turning the corner home, I suddenly saw the freak; he was standing right by our door. My heart thumped, and I immediately drew myself up. The freak didn't move. As usual, he had leaned his face on the doorjamb motionlessly, as if he were sniffing it.

The freak had seen a lot in his day, ragged, with a shabby motorcycle on three filthy wheels, painted a bluish color.

For some time now he had shown up every Sunday and stood in our doorway like an eyesore.

The owner of the motorcycle was a tractor driver from the nearby collective farm, a *jigit*[11] named Karatay. Although, of course, the word jigit hardly applied to that wrinkled, bearded fellow.

I hated that run-down motorcycle just as much as I disliked Karatay. After all, the damned thing was what brought its master to us.

As I had learned, a year earlier, Karatay's wife had died. After he lost his wife, he was free, and being free, he decided to marry again. Of course, the question arose here: to whom? And then the ass-like hopes and feelings of Karatay fixed on my beloved mother. You would think that all the other women had disappeared somewhere suddenly. That was why

---

[11] A *jigit* is a skilled and dashing horseman in Kazakh culture but the word can be used for any young man.

for some time, this filthy wreck had come "sniffing around" the doorway of our home on Sundays.

Of course, no one had asked my opinion and advice on this matter. Nevertheless, I was very mad at Karatay inside and said silently: "The hell my mother will marry you! Just you wait and see!"

Opening the door, I kicked the tire of the motorcycle hatefully. Indifferent to what was going on and obedient only to its owner, the vehicle jerked and then died again.

In the front room, my grandmother was whipping butter. Oh, how busy she always was! From early in the morning until the very dusk she bustled about in the house and the yard. Now my grandmother was whipping the butter so furiously that it seemed that just a little more and she would whip the bottom out of the bowl.

Her kerchief had fallen to her shoulders, her hair, grey from all that she had lived through, was damply glistening, so that a trace of the scent of sweat reached me. I kicked the ball aside which bounced off the wall and rolled into the corner, and headed into the room determinedly.

"Hey, where are you going looking like that? There are guests," Grandmother said, interrupting her chore.

What a strange person she was, still and all! Did she really not think I didn't know who was sitting in our house?

"So what if there are guests?"

No doubt my voice sounded very loud. Well, let him hear!

I tore the door open and went in. Karatay and Mama were sitting as usually across from each other at the dinner table by the window and talking. They glanced at me. From Karatay's face, I realized that he wasn't very happy at my arrival. Worse, my mother's stern look from under her knit brows let me know that she had not liked my stormy entrance at all.

With the same determined expression, I turned to the bookshelf which was in the far corner, and at that moment behind my back, Karatay's mocking voice resounded.

"Hey, Kozhatay[12], where's your 'hello'?"

I recalled how Mama had told me many a time that you must say hello first to an adult, or otherwise you will be terribly ill-bred.

"Hello," I said curtly, fulfilling this obligatory procedure.

Having burst into the room where the adults were sitting without any purpose, I was now forced to find myself something to do. I went up to the bookshelf and began to rifle through the newspapers and journals laying on the bottom shelf with a preoccupied expression. God knows what I stubbornly sought there and couldn't find. And although my back was to Mama and Karatay, my ears keenly caught each of their words.

"Yes, this spring has been rainy," Karatay said after a brief silence. "The wheat at our Comintern farm is already up to your waist. It rustles

---

12 A diminutive form of the name "Kozha."

like the sea, and grows with every day. If only the fall would come without downpours and hail, we could be reassured about the grain."

I immediately understood that the conversation had been interrupted because of me and Karatay was now chattering all sorts of nonsense. If only not to be silent.

Without straightening my back, I continued to sort through the papers leisurely, thinking about what Karatay would say next.

"That would be great," my flustered mother said, supporting him.

It seemed you could hear in her voice: "Oh, Karatay, my son is not so easy to deceive. He senses everything and understands!"

Silence hung again. Several minutes passed. Suddenly, my mother asked me sternly:

"Son, what are you digging around in there for?"

Her words lashed me like a belt woven of six reeds. Especially the word "son," which sounded cold and dry. Usually my mother always called me by my name. But now she had pronounced the word "son" as if she was speaking to a stranger. It was as if she had shook me and said, stop your stupid ruse and don't eavesdrop on adults! I understood everything and grabbing the first magazine to hand, I slipped out of the room.

That day, Karatay was at our house less time than usual. After a little bit, he came out after me. Before leaving, he cheerfully said good-bye to Grandma, joked with me and without paying any attention to my dislike, gave me a friendly slap on the back. It had happened before that Karatay would offer me a ride on his motorcycle around the aul, hoping to win my affection.

But this time, it was all different. He left the room with a downcast expression, his face, already swarthy, darkened. I ate my dinner at a low round table in the front room. Karatay silently slid an indifferent gaze over my face and headed toward the door. More likely out of necessity rather than from the heart, he forced himself to say as he left, turning toward Grandma, "Good bye, *Baybishe*[13]" – and without further delay, he went outside. In a minute, we could hear the cough of the motor and then a deafening, intermittent crack which sounded like the firing of several guns. The crack of this round wouldn't die down but ricocheted around the yard and down the street far into the distance, where it fell silent.

---

[13] *Babyishe* – a respectful form of address to the hostess, to an older woman.

CHAPTER THREE

In Which You Learn About Some of My Thoughts and the Tracks on the Sand

Why hide it, I was happy at the hasty retreat of Karatay and really wanted him never to come back again from that day on.

Did my mother really want to marry him? That couldn't be. To marry a complete stranger...an old man, and with such a prickly beard...oh, no, she could never marry him. And really, no matter how handsome he would be, why would Mama want a strange man? Thank God, Mama, Grandma and I were getting along not so badly, just the three of us. We were well fed and dressed. Soon I would graduate from school and enter university. I would become a writer. And then I, Mama and Grandma, if she would be still alive them, would understand what real happiness was.

I really wanted to tell Mama about this, but how? It was awkward somehow to start a conversation on this topic. No, my mother couldn't dare take such a stupid step. Most likely she simply respected Karatay. Of course she would explain to Karatay that she had a nearly-grown son, and tell him firmly that she didn't plan to get married at all. But the problem was that Karatay himself didn't want to see or understand anything. He followed Mama everywhere, like a shadow. Oh, those annoying, shameless men!

No, it couldn't be that my mother would get married at all. This was simply impossible. She would never abandon us; after all, she was such an intelligent and well brought-up person. It was just for this character of hers that everyone in the aul from small to great treated her with great respect. Otherwise, why would they have elected her the second time in a row as a deputy of the district workers' council of deputies?

All of these thoughts of course came to mind only after I had my fill of dinner. It's hard to think when your stomach is growling from hunger.

Deciding to have a swim after all, I headed to the river.

The sun already hung low at the very horizon, but the heat had still not passed. I felt the burning heat baking the back of my head and shoulders. I gazed down at the tilled pastures spread out in the valley and saw above it, like a heating plate, an immense, endless, mirage. Across the field along a narrow, darkening road, Karatay's motorcycle chugged along, spewing up high to the sky a pillar of dust.

The hot sun apparently didn't even spare the river. It had grown noticeably more shallow. When there were high waters, the river would become as blue as the sky. Yes, in fact, the girls had been swimming here recently and likely among them was Zhanar. Zhanar. What a pretty name! You simply had to get to know this girl. She is perfectly worthy of becoming one of the main characters of this tale.

She and I are in the same class. And it has to be said that first, Zhanar is the smartest girl in the glass and second, she is the prettiest. Especially when she puts on her red beret. In those minutes she looks like a pretty flower. And you should hear what kind of voice she has when she sings! And she dances so well, too! How she puts on a *tyubiteyka*[14] with peacock feathers and begins to dance the *Kamazhay*[15] – you simply can't take your eyes off her! She is quite a real artist! Besides, Zhanar is the best student in the class, she has straight A's.

Just try to say after all that that she can't be one of the main heroines of this tale.

When I think of Zhanar, it's as if my soul blossoms.

And let our class leader Maykanova scold me and think I'm a bad and undisciplined pupil. The day will come when I choose the right moment and tell Zhanar about my sacred dream, and share the secret which for now I hide in the depths of my soul. Then she will understand who I am. "Oh, it turns out that is how he is, Kozha! Of course, sooner or later his talent will definitely manifest himself," she will think.

Oh, if it were only like this: a person would be born already as an adult, would complete his business fully, and later turn into a child. I wonder what Maykanova would think of me then? Most likely she would think approximately like this: "Once Kozha was a famous writer, his name was known to the entire world. And now somehow it's awkward to scold him and lecture him, you have to respect a writer, after all!"

Unfortunately, in life, everything is constructed differently. First you are born into the world as a helpless baby. No one cares what you will grow up to be. Every other person lectures you on morality and orders you what to think, not trying to understand what is in your soul.

Some little thing – and immediately they raise a hue and cry:

"Kozha, you're awful!"

"Kozha, you're a hooligan!"

The sloping, sandy beach was empty. I felt bad that besides me, none of the other kids had come to swim. It wasn't very interesting to splash in the water by myself. I went along the shore and suddenly saw footprints from somebody's bare feet on the wet sand. "Perhaps, those are Zhanar's

---

[14] A *tyubiteyka* is an embroidered skull cap common in Central Asia.
[15] The *Kamazhay* is a national song for a native dance of Kazakhstan.

footprints?" the thought flashed through my mind. I bent down, peering at the footprints as if I could learn anything about who made them. Yes, likely these were Zhanar's foot prints. I raised my foot and, carefully measuring, stepped into the print. It turned out to be much smaller than my footprint. It seemed that Zhanar really had been here. I was filled with some sort of pleasant feeling, and without moving from the spot, froze in that strange and awkward pose.

CHAPTER FOUR

In Which Zhantas is Given a Trip to Pioneer Camp and I Am Not and How I Got Mad

After my morning tea, I took my time getting to the school athletic field. I had my ball squeezed under my arm. The day before, our team Spartak had lost to Kayrat with the score 7:5. Today we had to get our revenge on them no matter what. As the captain of the team, I was especially primed for victory and was internally preparing myself for the match.

Zhantas met me at the school. He had some kind of white piece of paper with a violet stamp in his hand. As I came up closer to him, Zhantas slapped me in the nose with his paper and grinning, said:

"Black Kozhe, guess what this is?"

"I don't know. What is it?" I said, not understanding.

"This is a voucher for the camp. We are going to camp this summer, and you're going to stay back in the aul and chase dogs!"

I wanted to teach Zhantas a lesson for his overly-sharp tongue, but I decided at first to find out some more.

"Who gave it to you?"

"Maykanova-*apay*,[16] who else? Don't worry, you're not in the list."

"I wonder why I'm not in the list?" I thought and asked:

"Where is she now?"

"In school. And what about it?" Zhantas grinned.

"Nothing," I replied. And pinching the sharp-tongued boy in the nose, so that he felt what it was like to mock others, I ran to the school.

Opening the door to the school, I flew in, hurried along the corridor, and gasping for breath from the run, burst into the teachers' room. Maykanova was sitting at the table and writing something. There was no one else but her in the room. She looked up at me in surprise and asked:

"What happened, Kadyrov? What's wrong with you?"

---

[16] Apay is a form of address to a woman.

"Give me a voucher for the camp, please!"

"This time, there isn't a voucher for you. You'll go next time."

"Why?"

"What do you mean, why? First of all, there aren't enough vouchers for all the pupils. Secondly, we sent to camp those who study the best and behave the best."

"So it turns out Zhantas is better them me, yeah?" I said, nearly choking from hurt.

Maykanova abruptly got up from the table as if something had poked her in the back.

"What, are you interrogating me?"

The teacher's grey eyes stared at me intently. I realized that Maykanova had gotten mad and now would not calm down very soon.

"If you don't want to give me one, then don't!" I cried and turning abruptly, I ran out of the teachers' room, slamming the door as hard as I could.

How could I calmly look at this obvious injustice? My blood was boiling. It meant that Zhantas – who loved to turn the kids against each other, who listened for hints while at the blackboard and who gossiped – was a better student than I? And the fact that my grades were higher than his, and that I tried to study even better didn't count, was that it?

"Kadyrov, get back here!" I heard the voice of Maykanova behind me. But I didn't even turn around.

"Kadyrov!"

I ran outside. Zhantas was standing with his back leaning on the chin-up bar, and chuckling, looking at me. Anger flashed in me with renewed strength.

"Well, did you get a voucher?" he asked snidely, blocking the way for me.

"I did!" I said defiantly.

"Well, let's see it!"

"Here!" I said, and slapped him roundly again on the nose.

Lying on the bed after dinner, I fell to thinking. What I had done in school today with the teacher was rude on my part. Of course, she was clearly wrong, giving the voucher to Zhantas and not me. That's what in fact set me off. But whatever you say, Maykanova was still and all the teacher, and moreover, our class leader. Well, alright then! Now vacation was coming, school was over, what could she do to me? And what might change in three months? Perhaps, in the new school year, we should have another class leader…Then I wouldn't go to Maykanova even on a cannon shot.

How amazing life is organized! There are people it seems in the world who can't get along with each other no matter what. It seemed that Maykanova and I were exactly such people. Our clashes began back in the fall, at that very same time when she came to us to work as a teacher. And it happened as follows. When I found out that the sale of textbooks and notebooks had begun, I asked my grandmother for money and hurried as fast as my legs would carry me to the store. The school sale was really at its height. There were an unusual number of people packed into the store, and the end of the line stretched out the door down the street.

I stood for a bit, thinking what to do, and decided to try to get inside. After all, those who were at the end of the line might not get a textbook. To go later, and borrow the books from first one classmate and then another, was that really necessary? No, whatever the case, you had to have your own textbooks. I even made up a proverb on the topic: "Whoever has his books together has a mood like sunny weather!".

Sidling my way through the crowd, I was getting ready to clip in, when suddenly a short, combative grey-eyed woman blocked my path.

"Where are you going? Now get back in line!" she said sternly.

And here my cursed tongue lied against my own will.

"I'm not here for the textbooks, I came for sugar!"

I dropped that line evidently because I saw how people were freely come and going to the counter in the back where there was produce.

The woman stepped aside and let me through with an imperturbable expression and headed to the produce counter. But as you can imagine, I really didn't need any sugar right then. I needed the fifth-grade textbooks. I slipped along the counter and squeezing between people in the crowd, began to make my way to the place where they were handing out the textbooks and workbooks. Just a little bit more – and I would have reached my goal. Suddenly, I felt somebody's hand grabbing me by the back of the neck. I turned and saw the same grey-eyed stranger.

"You're lost. The sugar is sold on the other side," she said.

"What does it matter to you, let me go!" I broke free from her grip and suddenly landed right at the counter.

"Don't give any books to the boy in the grey cap, he cut in line!" the woman shouted to the clerk.

No sooner did she finish the phrase than your quick-thinking Kozheken[17] swiped the gray cap from his head and turned into a shaven-headed dark-skinned boy.

While the kids at the counter babbled something, vying with each other to ask me something, without a word, I stuck 50 rubles[18] into the clerk's hand. After getting the textbooks and notebooks, I quickly headed to the exit. The grey-eyed stranger once again grabbed me by the shoulder at the door (oh, her fingers were tough!).

"Oh, how shameless you are! What class are you in?!" she said, shaking me.

However, obviously I had no intention of telling her anything about myself.

Several days later, the new school year began. And guess what! Grabbing some papers under my arm, and vigorously clicking her high-

---

[17] Kozheken – respectful form of the name "Kozha".

[18] 50 rubles in the old currency.

heel shoes, into our classroom walked that very grey-eyed young woman with whom I had clashed with in the store.

If you could see how sad the face of poor Kozheken became then! I quickly pulled myself together, however, and decided not to let on. Maybe she wouldn't recognize me?

The new teacher welcomed us at the start of the school year and introduced herself. Her name was Sabira Maykanova.

"I will conduct your classes in the Kazakh language, and at the same time, will be your class leader," she announced.

The last piece of news made an even greater impression on Kozheken.

"Well, dear fellow, hang on," I told myself.

Maykanova opened up the ledger and calling out one last name of the students after another, she began to get to know us. My turn came.

"Kadyrov!"

"Here!"

Maykanova raised her eyes and staring at me, said:

"I think we're already acquainted?"

I shrugged my shoulders and smiled vaguely.

"Perhaps."

"Sit down," Maykanova commanded in a tone not boding anything well.

From that day on, Maykanova perceived any offense of mine, even the most minor, with hostility. How many times she dragged me to the principal's office just that winter! It ended with a "four"[19] for me in behavior.

I didn't like any of this, of course.

---

[19] The Soviet grading system had points from 1-5, with 5 the highest mark.

CHAPTER FIVE

In Which You Learn How I Played *Shashki*[20] with Zhanar and about the Magic Dream Bird.

Two days later, a lot of the kids went off to Pioneer[21] camp with a cheerful racket.

Burning with envy, I remained in the aul. After noon, the brigadier came to our house.

"Black Kozhe, are you home?" he asked through the open door.

"Yes, I am," I replied and went outdoors.

"Get your clothes and bedding and be prepared. You're going to the haying. All the children who were left in the aul will go there today. You'll help us bring in the harvest."

"I won't go!" I said.

"Why?"

"I am a bad, undisciplined student and am not fit for anything."

Learning about the reason for my upset, the brigadier cheerfully exclaimed,

"What a thing to worry about! And you, a *jigit*! What's so great about that camp, tell me, please? You'll see the most interesting stuff at the haying. We'll make all the conditions there for a lot of fun!" he began fervently agitating me.

Agitate or not, but Kozheken, when necessary, knows how to stand his ground. Furthermore, I knew that Maykanova was going to the haying. That was all I needed! No way, I wouldn't set foot anywhere Maykanova was going. Let me at least get a rest from her during the summer.

I don't remember if I told you that my mother works at the collective farm as a dairy maid? So several days ago, the farm migrated to the *jaylyau*.[22] I

---

[20] *Shashki* is a board game similar to checkers or draughts.

[21] Pioneers was the name of the Soviet youth organization for elementary school age children.

[22] The jaylyau is a summer pasture usually high in the mountains where semi-nomadic people would take their livestock to graze in the spring and summer before the winter.

hadn't been at the *jaylyau* for several years, and wouldn't it be better for me to head out there? For that, I just needed transportation. But where could I get it?

Asking the brigadier was useless, he wouldn't give it to me anyway. Oh, it would be wonderful to have my own horse! You could go anywhere you wanted, whenever you felt like it! No wonder the Kazakhs say, "A horse is the wings of a *jigit*."

But where could I get a horse?

Bah! Was that really a problem? After all, the times were different now. Private property had long ago been liquidated and it turned out that the livestock that belonged to the collective farm belonged to me, too. That meant I could take any horse and go on my way. Each of the collective farm activists had several horses that they groomed and cared for so that even a fly couldn't land on it. In the summer, the masters let them out to the *jaylyau*, where they would graze on the succulent grasses, and in the winter, would guard them carefully, chasing away wolves. Did these people pay anything to the collective farm for these services or not? Most likely they didn't pay anything. My father, Kadyrov, worked at the collective farm from the very first days of its founding as a blacksmith, and my mother worked as a dairy maid. Did I really not have the right to use one of the horses for a day?

Thus, the decision was taken. In a little while, Kozheken would head to the coastal meadow where the herd of horses would wander lazily, choosing what looked best and in the cool of the night, travel upward in the direction of the *jaylyau*. And then let even the brigadier or even Maykanova herself try to find any trace of me.

I ate dinner and went outside. The twilight was already growing thick and all around everything was gradually plunging into the night-time murk. Wrapped in the tender night-time coolness, I sat on the low log gates, like a patient brood hen. My thoughts were about Zhanar. If I went that night to the jaylyau then I wouldn't see her very soon. How I would miss her!

Sometimes I asked myself the same question: "Why am I thinking about Zhanar all the time? And why am I so agitated when I don't see her?" Perhaps it was that very thing…about which the grown-ups talk and write in books?

I had only to remember this "secret" word and I would immediately shudder. What if Maykanova found out about it? It was terrible to think what would await me then.

"Ah, Kadyrov! You didn't manage to grow out of diapers and you're already in love with a girl?! Look at him! Admit it, who taught you this outrage?" What a scandal would be kicked up all over the school.

It was for that very reason that not only didn't I strike up a conversation with Zhanar; I was even afraid to approach her.

The house where my classmate lived was at the head of a street not far from the river. Her father, Balabek, worked as a brigadier. Her mother had gone to a rest home in the Crimea. At Zhanar's house, there was still her grandmother – a strict old lady who for some reason didn't like me. I took a stick to hand and, pretending to limp, headed toward their house. If I could at least see Zhanar from a distance, even that would enable me to endure the separation. And perhaps she would meet me along the road? Then I would tell her that I was going away to the *jaylyau*. Let her know where I was, and sometimes think of me. I wonder if Zhanar thought about me even rarely, or not?

At Zhanar's house, there was one more creature besides the grandmother which I feared as well. That was a furious, cursed black dog. He was so mean that he would hurl himself even at a man on horseback. If the dog didn't sit on a leash, but was freely running around the yard, then not a single person could walk by that house calmly.

To my satisfaction, the dog turned out to be tied up. You could hear how she angrily barked intermittently at somebody, and strained against the leash, clanging the chain. I had barely drew up to the wooden fence when the door to the house was flung open and Zhanar ran into the yard.

"Aktos, down! Sit!" she cried at the dog.

A female voice could be heard from behind the gate.

"Zhanar-*zhan*[23], is your grandmother home?"

"No, she went to the bird farm not long ago to visit Grandfather Syunbay and hasn't got back yet," came the answer.

Learning that Zhanar was home alone, I was terribly thrilled and decided to talk with her no matter what.

"Zhanar!" I called, when she had returned to the house with the same run. My voice sounded loud and resonant as if a person had shouted who was either frightened or who had suddenly found some precious metal on the ground.

Startled, Zhanar halted. Above the front door an electric lightbulb burned, casting a bright circle in front of the house. Not realizing where the voice had come from, she looked around in confusion and at last saw me.

"Hello, Zhanar!"

The expression of surprise on Zhanar's face changed to a smile. She ran to the fence, grabbing the sharpened ends of the pickets with her hands, and turned to face me.

"Hello, Kozha. What are you doing here?" she asked.

"I'm going away to the jaylyau tonight."

"To your mother's?"

"Yes. And why aren't you in camp?"

"I will help my grandmother at home until my mother gets back. Maykanova-*apay* promised to give me a voucher for the next season" Zhanar replied, and immediately added: "Kozha, my grandmother isn't home. Let's go and play *shashki*."

---

[23] *Zhan* is a term of affection.

I nearly jumped for joy on the spot, as if wings sprouted from me. I flew to the fence and in a flash I was on the other side. At the same time, the black shaggy dog hurled at me with a loud bark, dragging its chain. Making a frightened expression, I grabbed Zhanar hard by the hand and pressed close to her. The chain was short and did not let the dog get close to the house. Shoulder to shoulder, we ran into the house.

"Do you play well?" Zhanar asked.

"No, not very," I replied reluctantly, although in fact I would beat almost all my friends.

We sat across from each other, laying out the board, and began to play.

I couldn't tear my eyes off the sweet face of Zhanar who was so close to me. I kept admiring her beautiful, shiny, black fluffy hair, which cascaded to her shoulders, and didn't notice how I lost the first round.

I wasn't offended. On the contrary, seeing Zhanar's happy eyes, in my heart I was happy with my loss.

In the second round, I tried to play more attentively than in the first. You can't keep losing to a girl all the time. However, in three or four moves, Zhanar knocked over three of my *shashki*.

"Now, that's something!" I cried, and slapping myself in the cheek, stared at the board in surprise. The first loss had brought others along with it, the game hadn't settled down, and soon I was once again losing.

"Hurray! Hurray!" Zhanar rejoiced even more than the last time. Now my vanity was awoken.

"That's nothing, I'll win now," I said confidently.

"And if you lose, what will you be?"

"Whatever you say I should be, I'll be!"

"You will be the greatest bragger in the entire world."

"Alright."

The third round began rather lively. In the very first minutes, each one of us lost two shashki. But after awhile, the balance of the game was disrupted. Once again I missed a few times and Zhanar got the upper hand.

"Just you wait! Let's see how you win!" my rival said happily, anticipating her impending success.

Now all my hope lay on a *shashka*[24] that was on the far right edge. Moving it along, I finally was able to bring it out to the king. "Well, hang on! How I will knock yours out now!" I thought to myself.

And at that very moment, on the field of battle, something amazing happened. Clever Zhanar gave up a half-forgotten *shashka* to me, but meanwhile led another toward the queen. But that apparently seemed not enough for her; she knocked out my three remaining "warriors" with her newly-appeared queen.

---

[24] A *shashka* is a game piece in shashki, a game like checkers.

"Hurray! You lost, you braggart, Kozha! Now I will call you Braggart Kozha."

"Wait…how…how did that happen?" I could not understood what hit me.

"Look. You knocked out my *shashka*? You did. And then I took this one and went to the queen. And then I went here…here…and here. Oh, you Braggart Kozha! And you kept telling me you'd win!"

"Wait. I still have one king left."

"And what of it? What can it do?"

"Let's see. You haven't won yet. Whose turn is it now, mine?"

On the board standing against my only king were four of Zhanar's *shashki*. One of them was a queen. The other three could also without hindrance go to the queen. The further course of events did not leave any doubt. Four black threatening queens would likely surround me and like a pack of wolves throw themselves on my *shashka* and destroy it. I so keenly imagined this scene that without noticing it myself, I moved the queen along the diagonal to the furthest corner away from her pieces. This was the only way out for me.

Guessing my trick, Zhanar exclaimed:

"Oh, you coward! You are frightened, yes? Let's see where you're going next!"

There really was nowhere for me to go. The danger awaited me from both sides. If I moved away from her just a bit, I would immediately die. Thus, there was nothing for me to do but to slide from one end of the diagonal to the other – back and forth, back and forth – not changing my course.

"That's not how you play! Get off that road!" Zhanar said, indignantly.

"This is my right. If I want, I will get off. If I don't want, I won't get off."

"No, get off it!"

"I won't!"

"Then you lose."

"No, I didn't lose."

"You lose!"

"I didn't lose."

"You lose! From this day on I will call you Braggart Kozha!"

Now Zhanar and I fought in earnest. She continued to claim that I had lost; I maintained that I had not lost and demanded that we play to the end.

"In that case, take away the queen!" Zhanar held her ground.

"I don't think so!" I said, refusing.

"I won't play with you!" Zhanar cried suddenly and frowning, began to collect the game pieces.

"Well, then don't," I said defiantly.

A dog barked in the yard and immediately quieted down. The gate squeaked open.

"My grandmother's probably home!" Zhanar hurled herself to the door. I followed her outside.

Zhanar's grandmother was walking from the gate to the house.

"Oh, my sweetie, you're sitting home alone?" she said tenderly to her grand daughter and then saw me. "And who's this? Kozha, is it?" the old lady asked with obvious dislike.

"Yes," Zhanar replied, throwing a hurt look at me.

"What was he doing here?"

"He and I were playing shashki."

"Sonny, go home," the grandmother said to me. "Zhanar-*zhan*[25], see the boy off, so the dog doesn't bite him."

I thought it might be better just to jump over the fence and not go to the gate along the entire fence, irritating the already-angry dog. Let me be unlucky today in *shashki* but then Zhanar could see once again what a good athlete I was. Now there was a convenient opportunity for this, and I decided to make use of it and do at least something she'd like.

"Good-bye," I said, and easily ran to the fence. When I reached it, I jumped over and…No, whatever you say, I didn't know, I hadn't guessed that it would be exactly here that such a disgrace awaited me! Do you want to know what happened? What happened is that one of my pant legs snagged on the sharp end of the picket and I clattered to the ground. I fell hard, it was very painful, but for good reason do they say that sometimes, shame is more terrible than death. I immediately scrambled to my feet and without a backward glance darted away, hearing the loud, cheerful laughter of Zhanar and her grandmother.

* * *

"*Yapyray*, I shouldn't have offended Zhanar. And why did I suddenly act up like that? Of course, my foolish, stubborn nature was to blame. It was always betraying me! Oh, what would it have cost me to go on the diagonal and lose? Nothing would have happened to me had I done that," I fretted with belated regret. Before my eyes once again arose the hurt face of Zhanar. Forgive me, forgive me, please. Zhanar, I was wrong." I recalled how I pretended to be afraid of the dog, and grabbed Zhanar's hand, and once again sensed a pleasant warmth in my chest. I squeezed my fingers as if Zhanar's hand once again lay in my palm.

All kinds of thoughts roiled around in my head. I'll finish school, I'll go serve in the army. Zhanar will likely enter the institute. Then I will write her many wonderful letters, even in verse. Without a doubt. Zhanar will reply to me. And perhaps she'll begin her letters with, "Dear Kozha! How pleasant that sounds indeed! Closing my eyes, I continued to dream…

---

[25] The suffix *zhan* added to a name is a sign of affection.

...It was night. It was pitch-black all around me. A cold rain was falling, incessantly and monotonously...Heavy, dark clouds swam chaotically around the thunderous sky, which looked like rebellious waves. From time to time, peals of thunder rolled through the sky, and lightning flashed brightly, blinding the eyes. On the shore of the bubbling, capricious mountain river, ignoring the frolicsome elements and firmly gripping a weapon in his hand, stood a vigilant border guard at his post. That soldier, courageously performing his military duty, was of course me.

Perhaps, right that night, exploiting the bad weather, a cunning enemy would aim at our country and try to encroach on our scared Soviet border. But I was prepared to battle him to the last drop of blood. Then I saw the enemies' tanks moving in our direction, sweeping away powerful trees in their wake, one after another coming closer to the border. I lay under a bush and prepared my anti-tank grenades, watching the mammoths looming ahead carefully. Soon, the forward tank was nearby. I rose up and hurled my first grenade at it. It hit the target perfectly and exploded. The second, third and all the rest of the tanks met the same fate. The defeated invaders were mowed down at the very border, never having put a foot on our land.

My fame flew about the whole country, of course. I suppose they even printed my photograph in the paper. How Zhanar will be agitated then!

After I received the title of Hero, with a sparkling medal on my chest, finally I return home. A huge crowd of people meet me at the bridge with bright bouquets of flowers in their hands. Among them I see Zhanar right away. As if she had pined away like the story of the separated lovers Kozy and Bayan,[26] we would throw ourselves at each other with outstretched arms.

"Zhanar!"

"Kozha!"

Now a group of teachers were coming toward me with Akhmetov, the principal of the school. "You're great, Kozha! You're a real *jigit*! It's too bad we didn't know how brave you were, we shouldn't have scolded you. Forgive us," Akhmetov would say. "Yes, you yelled at me too often... Especially Maykanova-*apay*."

Not daring to approach me, Maykanova would stand to the side with a guilty expression. "Why so shy, come closer," I would say. Stepping hesitantly, she would approach me and say, "Forgive me, Kozha...Likely you haven't forgotten how I didn't give you a voucher for the Pioneers' camp?" "Yes, I remember that." "Forgive me, forgive me dear Kozhatay!"

What should I do? Forgive her? No, I could forgive anyone but Maykanova, because she had offended me too deeply. I call Akhmetov aside and tell him to fire Maykanova from the school. That's enough, I think. And just let Akhmetov try not to obey the wish of a Hero of the Soviet Union!

---

[26] Kozy-Korpesh and Bayan-Sulu were heroes of a Kazakh national epic lovers' tale.

CHAPTER SIX

In Which I Speak of My Grandmother, How I Tried to Steal a Horse and My Meeting with Sultan

I sat home and read a book, waiting for the hour when the aul would go to sleep. Noticing that Grandma was making up my bed, I said:

"You don't have to make up my bed. I'm going to the jaylyau today."

"What do you mean – today?" said Grandma, surprised. "So late?"

"Yes. It's too hot during the day. And it's best of all to ride a horse at night."

"Where did you find a horse?"

"The main thing isn't where, the main thing is that I found it and the horse is all ready," I replied calmly.

"Oh, you silly thing, have you got up to some prank again?"

"What prank? You always suspect me of something."

"How can I not suspect you when you can't go by a single day in peace?

Grandma came up to me – and for the nth time! – began lecturing me.

"My little sun,[27] behave yourself, don't touch anybody and don't poke your nose where it doesn't belong. Keep in mind that besides me, no one can stand your pranks. And listen to my advice: live quietly, sonny, live quietly. Don't cause other people unpleasantness."

Strange people, these adults. No matter whom you pick, each one tries to teach you morality, annoying behavior – teaching and styling themselves geniuses. How they love to teach – behave this way, not that way, do this, don't do that. But look at them themselves! Don't the adults themselves sometimes do the nastiest and stupidest things? Who is it that steals, and then goes to court? Adults. It's among adults that you find scandal-mongers, skin-flints and gossipers. Who stages drunken rows in their families, torments their wives and children? Adults.

---

[27] "My little sun" is a term of endearment.

How right it would be if they first disciplined themselves and then explained to their children what is good and what is bad.

My grandmother was also a rather interesting person. Throughout the whole aul, you would hardly find someone who knew the most diverse everyday living and household tips. Despite this, in many things, she was as naïve as a child. Of course, her naiveté was explained above all by her lack of education. No matter how hard I tried, for example, I have never been able to get it through to her that the earth is round. We argued for a long time until finally, tired of me, she waved her hand.

"Go away from me! You're round, and not the earth. Go away, and don't trouble my head with all kinds of stupidities!"

Sometimes, she and I would start arguing about God.

"If there is no God on earth, then who created this world?" Grandma would ask.

"No one created it, it emerged by itself."

"What, you godless creature, did you watch this yourself?"

"No, I didn't, but I read it in books."

"But who created the people?"

"People came from apes."

"Phew, you blabbermouth! Stop spouting nonsense and go back into the forest to your ancestors then!"

That was usually how our scientific discussions with Grandma ended up.

Deciding that the aul residents had already gone to their homes, I went outside. In the dark shed, there was a riding crop in the spot I had prepared. I groped it with my hand, took it down from the nail and then squeezed it under my arm so that it wouldn't jingle. I headed between the high fields behind the house right to the river.

How wonderful it would be if I were going not alone now, but with Zhanar! I vividly imagined such a picture: the tender, velvet night had fallen on the silent, endless vistas. A dusty road disappears somewhere into the distance, and a pair slowly rides along it. Zhanar and I, of course, would speak of our cherished dreams, about the future…

The riding horses of our aul would descend to the coastal meadow at night, so that's where I headed. Finally I saw the darkening silhouette of a horse on the outside of the herd. Coming closer, I recognized the bay mare Alshanbay. On her legs were massive iron chains, dangling disobediently like Alshanbay herself. Her colt quietly munched the grass next to his mother. Nearby there were two more horses. I went up to them. At last God had sent me good fortune! Imagine that it would happen, that I would end up next to the ginger-mane ambler of the chairman of the collective farm himself. I had long dreamt of riding on this stallion even once. And now the long-awaited moment had come when I could realize my dream. The front legs of the horse were hobbled. He wasn't the most docile of horses as I could hear coming closer – he snorted and pricked up his ears in alarm.

"Whoa, whoa," I said to soothe the stallion and tried to stroke his neck. But he got his back up, waved his tale and once again pricked up his ears.

"Hey! What are you doing, silly," I cried sharply, imitating the horse-herder Satybay, then once again tenderly continuing, "Whoa, whoa, sweetie!"

It was all in vain. The ginger ambler kept not letting me near him. Shout at him or not – it made no difference. The horse glared at me in alarm and it seemed that he was about to lie down.

Then I got a burst of stubbornness which sits in me like the devil. "Just you wait, you obstinate creature! I'll get you to dance! Once I have you under me, I'll show you who's boss!" I decided not to back down at any price to get what I want. If only I could grab hold of his mane, it would go easier.

I circled the horse for a long time and finally, catching the right moment, hurled myself at him and grabbed his thick mane. The stallion snorted in fright, lurched to the side and broke into a trot.

I dangled at his side, tightly gripping his mane, my feet flying over the ground, only touching them for a moment. But I didn't let go of my grip. What a wild horse he was! He continued to trot around and didn't intend to stop. After a while, I suddenly felt my fingers weakening and my grip slacking. I flew off to the side head over heels, and the horse, turning around, picked up its hind legs and kicked me. The blow from the hoof hit my right thigh. Like a puppy who had stepped on hot coals, I wailed in pain and rolled over the earth. Fortunately, the blow was a side-swipe. Had he kicked me directly, who knows, my bone might have really been injured.

Suddenly, a voice sounded above me.

"Hey, who's here? Who are you?"

I jerked and immediately fell silent. Someone in a cap was leaning over me. He had the crop in his hand. Looking up, I recognized Sultan. He bent down and peered at me for a while and then suddenly exclaimed:

"Hey, it's Black Kozhe! What's wrong with you? Why are you rolling around on the ground?"

"The horse kicked me."

"Which horse?"

"That one," I said pointing at the ginger ambler.

"Where did he kick you? Are your bones alright?"

"I think they are," I replied carefully, extending my leg.

"Well, let's take a look," said Sultan, and dropping the crop to the ground, grabbed my leg.

"*Oybay*,[28] careful!" I yelped in fright.

"What a coward you are!" Sultan said, looking at me mockingly. "How you fear for your precious life! Wait a minute, don't jerk around, you

---

[28] A Kazakh exclamation of shock or surprise.

won't die! Why, there's no break here, it's just a small bruise. As soon as you get home, put some ribwort plantain on it, it will disappear like magic. And here I thought somebody was bit by a snake. What, didn't you know how mad this ginger is? Why did you go after him?"

"I just…was going by him and he kicked me."

"What a fool!" Sultan began laughing at me. "What, are you blind, you don't see a horse in front of you? It's not a fly!"

Not knowing what to answer, I pretended that I was very busy with my sore leg and once again began to moan and groan.

"Get up and don't whine like your leg is broken," Sultan told me, and without paying attention to my groans, grabbed me by the hand and forced me to get up.

"Now, try making a step. Another one. You see, I told you, you didn't break any bones at all. Imagine, the horse kicked you a bit. You don't break your legs from that. Don't be afraid, you won't die. Stop lying around, let's go. And don't limp, walk normally!"

Sultan was about three years older than me. His father, Sugur, was the horse-herder. He himself dropped out of school several years ago and ever since, like an ancient knight, rode first one horse, then another he liked from among his father's herd, and rode around the steppe. Sometimes he disappeared for a long time from sight and then once again appeared in the aul. Allah alone knew where he went off to and what he did.

"Where have you come from?" I asked him.

"From the *jaylyau*."

"How is it there at the *jaylyau*?"

"Oh, don't ask!" Sultan rolled his eyes. "It's wonderful! If you could see how high the grass is. It's up to your waist!"

"I'd like to go there, but I have nothing to go on," I sighed.

"Let me take you with me," Sultan proposed. "I'm going back there tomorrow morning."   "How?" I said, surprised. "Do you have a free horse?"

"It's not your business. Get ready and wait for me in the morning. Do you have a saddle?"

"I do."

"Great. It's a deal."

Sultan accompanied me to the doors of our house and asked suddenly,

"Black Kozhe, tell me, if I ask you to go with me to a certain place, will you go?"

"Where?" I wondered, but Sultan, looking me over, shook his head.

"No, with you limping like this, you'll get into some sort of trouble. Alright, for now. I'm off. Be ready tomorrow morning, okay?"

CHAPTER SEVEN

In which Sultan and I Put Two Saddles on One Horse and How Sultan Taught Me to Smoke and How This All Ended.

In the morning, I had barely managed to drink some tea when Sultan road up to our house on a horse.

"Black Kozhe, are you home?" I heard him call.

"Yes, yes."

"Well, are you ready?"

"I'm ready."

"Bring out the saddle."

I took the saddle and came outside. Sultan was sitting upright on a sinewy light-brown three-year-old horse with a black mane and tail, an important expression on his face. To my surprise, he didn't have in tow any other ride, even an old, wretched nag.

"Where's the horse for me?" I asked disappointedly.

"And what's this, do you think?" Sultan replied, surprised, slapping his horse on the flank.

"Saddle up."

"Where?"

"Here, behind me. You don't know this stallion very well. You can be sure he'll take us not only to the jaylyau but to Almaty itself."

"What, we're going to put two saddles on one horse?" I asked, surprised.

"Why are you so surprised? Everything will be fine, you'll see!"

To be honest, until that moment I had never seen Kazakhs who had saddled a horse with two saddles. Sultan's idea seemed to me in fact intriguing and interesting. I arranged the saddle behind him, pulled the straps and climbed up on the horse. At that moment my grandmother came outside.

"Oh, Lord, what's all this?" she cried and shielding her eyes from the sun, stared at us in amazement. "Oh, you pranksters, oh, you clever thing, what have you thought up now!" she said to Sultan.

I felt wonderful. It really was much more comfortable than without a saddle. Your legs didn't dangle because we each had our own stirrups.

Trotting along two or three streets, we reached the store and stopped near by. Throwing his leg over the horse's mane, Sultan jumped to the ground and handing me the reins, said:

"Here, hold this. Do you have any money?"

"Why?"

"How much?"

"Five rubles. Why?"

"Is that all? Well, alright, give them here."

How could I refuse Sultan, sitting on his horse? I slowly unbuttoned the button on my shirt pocket and reluctantly reached my hand in.

"Hey, what are you digging around in there for?"

How could I not dig, if there was a reason?

"Wait, for some reason, I can't find it."

"Maybe they're in another pocket?"

"No, they were in this one."

I took my time. In fact I had two crisp bills in my pocket, but I couldn't determine by just feel which one of them was the five-ruble note. Finally, I made up my mind and hoping for good luck, dragged out one of them. Oh, horror! As soon as I caught sight of the edge of the bill peeking out of my pocket, my heart sank. It turned out I had fished out the ten-ruble note.

"Hey, is that a tenner?" Sultan cried happily. "Oh, you sneak, Black Kozhe! You can't get by without being sneaky! Alright, if it's a tenner, it's a tenner, give it here!"

"I thought it was five rubles, but it turned out to be ten," I said in justification, trying to hide my disappointment.

No sooner had Sultan grabbed my ten-ruble note and disappeared into the store than I once again plunged my hand into my pocket where the second bill was still nestled and pulled it out. It was the five-ruble note. The very five rubles that had so let me down and covered me with shame. I was so angry that I wanted to tear them up to bits and throw them away. Looking at the already crumpled and dirty bill, I felt sorry for it and once again hid it in my pocket.

Sultan soon came out of the store, chewing on something. The pockets of his trousers were packed with something.

"What did you buy?" I asked.

"Some'hing for 'a woad," Sultan replied, barely turning over his tongue as he tried to say "the road," evidently.

He took the reins from my hands and once again mounted the horse.

"Let's go," I said, hurrying him. I didn't want Zhanar to see how I was sticking up on the horse behind Sultan's back.

We rode out of the aul, leaving behind us the last of the houses. Sultan fished two cookies out of the pocket of his trousers and handed one of them to me. Munching happily, we slowly moved along the steppe road, the hooves of the tawny horse knocking hollowly on the rocky ground.

A little while later, Sultan turned back toward me and asked:

"Do you smoke?"

"No," I said.

Continuing to sit sideways, Sultan tugged the reins and pulled a pack of cigarettes out of his pocket, unsealed it, and handed it to me.

"Here, learn."

"No, smoke yourself," I said, refusing.

"How is it that you haven't learned to smoke until now?" Sultan tried to shame me. "Well, go on and learn, it's time now. Here, take one!"

I obediently took a cigarette out of the pack and stuck it in my mouth. Sultan lit a match. I lit the cigarette then furiously smoked, making one draft after another. My mouth filled with the bitter stench of smoke.

"Hey, you're not doing it right," Sultan reproached me, noticing how I was smoking. "Do people smoke like that? What good cigarettes you'll waste that way! Drag it in! Like this, do you see?" He drew a full mouth of smoke and then swallowed it.

How stupid children are sometimes! They know that some things are very harmful but they are drawn to them like blind puppies. And now I was suddenly curious. I wonder what will happen if I swallow it? Well, let me try!

If you had such a misfortune happen to you, likely you will understand my state. Hardly had I filled my mouth full of smoke than that very second the terribly poisonous gas penetrated me and filled me entirely with a repulsive nausea. I choked, and started coughing loudly. Tears sprang to my eyes. Suddenly everything swam before my eyes and it seems I was about to fall over.

"*Oybay*, wait," I shouted to Sultan, and toppling over the horse, slid to the ground. I was terribly nauseous, but I couldn't throw up and only helplessly writhed at the edge of the road.

"Poor Black Kozhe! Likely you'll die three days before your time!" nasty Sultan said mockingly instead of feeling sorry for me. "What will I tell Millat-*apay* now? With what face will I appear before her? He couldn't at least get to the *jaylyau* and die there if he was taken so ill? But here there will be a great deal of bother with you!"

Ever since that day, not only do I not smoke, but I run away as soon as I smell that nasty, poisonous stench of tobacco.

CHAPTER EIGHT

In Which the Reader Meets Daulet, a New Hero of My Tale

With the same slow amble, the tawny horse brought us to the mountain valley in the afternoon. The weather here, like the nature all around us, was different than what was below on the plain. Here total silence reigned, even a fly couldn't be heard. From the valley, a pleasant coolness wafted out to greet us. All around, wherever you looked were varied fluffy grasses and bright flowers.

The long ride on horseback had tired me. It turns out that when you ride behind, you are shaken much more. I looked at Sultan. He sat in the saddle with a cap pulled down over his eyes, showing the back of his head, sun-burnt from the fiery sun. I couldn't wait to stretch out on the tender and soft grass, which was like velvet, next to a spring welling up nearby.

"Sultan, what if we take a little rest?" I asked my friend.

"Are you tired?"

"I'm thirsty."

"We'll go a little further and reach the shepherds' yurt where there will be plenty of *kumys*.[29] We'll take a rest there," replied Sultan.

And that's how it was. Cresting the next mountain range, we saw not far away off to the right a lonely yurt.[30] The *koshma*[31], worn and darkened with time, which was stretched over the yurt was topped with a new, white *tunduk*[32]. At the entrance, fresh *kurt*[33] was drying on a mat woven from chia. Flatbreads lay here and there around the yurt, and the pasture spread out nearby. It was clear from everything that we had come to an old post. Not far from the yurt, we saw two stallions on tethers. One of them, a grey stallion, was motionlessly splayed out over the ground, warming his

---

[29] *Kumys* is fermented mare's milk.
[30] A yurt is portable, round tent covered with skins or felt used as a home by nomads in the steppes of Central Asia.
[31] A *koshma* is a kind of rug covering a yurt.
[32] The *tunduk* is the opening at the top of the yurt where there is a lattice of the poles holding it up.
[33] *Kurt* is a kind of dried whey.

flank in the sun. The other had frozen still next to him, lowering its head as if it were listening to the ground.

"Thank God, soon we will drink our fill of *kumys*," said Sultan, cheering me, and directed the horse toward the yurt. Suddenly, three dogs sprang out to meet us, barking loudly and fiercely. One of them, a floppy-eared, white-chested hound the size of a yearling calf, ran up close, and, barking in hoarse bursts, began to throw himself at the horse, jumping almost up to his muzzle. The other, a mobile black bitch, as if she didn't want to let the horse near the house, bit on to his tail and pulled him back.

But the character of my *Sultekan*[34] was a lot worse than these dogs. He started waving his whip to the left and right, driving those dogs into a frenzy, and with an incredible noise, pulled up finally to the yurt and stopped at its doors.

At that moment, the flap that covered the entrance to the yurt drew aside and out came a bright, freckle-faced boy of about 11 or 12. He had a green border guard's cap on his head. It seemed it was a size too big for him and somebody's unskilled hand had gathered in the cap at the back and crudely sewn it with black thread.

Without paying attention to us, the boy quickly ran to a pole standing at the yurt and set about chasing the dogs away.

"Get out of here! Quickly now! Go to your mat, Alypsok, go!" he cried.

To my surprise, the enormous dog named Alypsok immediately obeyed its little master. Angrily yelling one last time, she looked up unhappily at us and did not hurry to leave. The other dogs disappeared behind her. Only then did the boy with the pole turn to us.

"Whose house is this?" asked the freckle-faced boy without dismounting.

"It's Zhumagul's house."

"And what does Zhumagul do?"

"Pastures sheep."

"Is anyone home?"

"No."

"Where's your mother?"

"She went to the aul which is over on that ridge there."

"Do you have any kumys?"

"No, there's no kumys. Some people were here recently and they drank it all up."

"What, there isn't anything left?"

"Nothing…left," the boy answered hesitantly.

"Why lie? What did you do with the *burdyuk*[35] with the kumys, hidden behind clothes and tied to the window of the yurt?"

"Who told you about that?"

"Zhumeken. We met him along the way with a flock of sheep. He said

<hr />

[34] *Sultekan* is a version of Sultan's name showing affection.
[35] A *burdyuk* is a skin bag.

it was under the clothes, that a *burdyuk* was hanging on the wall with *kumys* and that we should carefully, without spilling any, pour ourselves out a *piyala*[36] each and drink it," Sultan said calmly and quietly punched me in the knee so that I didn't give anything away.

His mouth agape, the boy froze in complete confusion. Likely Sultan's impromptu fiction hit the mark, and now he was tensely trying to think up how he should behave.

"It's time for us to take a break!" said Sultan and turned the horse toward the post. We dismounted, tied up the horse and headed toward the youth. The freckle-faced boy, still not moving from his spot, followed us with a silent gaze. It seemed he was consumed with doubt and didn't know how to act.

It was semi-dark and cool inside the yurt. Sultan, as if he were at the home of his closest relative, flopped down on the *tor*,[37] and taking advantage of the absence of the owner, lifted up the piles of clothing at the wall and looked underneath them. In fact there really was a fat *burdyuk* with *kumys* tied to the window.

The boy, uncertain as if he were afraid of something, came into the yurt and froze at the doorway. He was wearing a blue satin shirt which had grown shapeless from numerous washings. Its hem barely reached to the waist of his trousers, and his tan stomach, round as a ball, peeked out from underneath.

"Hey, what's your name?" asked Sultan.

"Daulet."

"What a pretty name you have! Daulet – the prettiest name on earth! My older brother is called Daulet, too."

As far as I knew, Sultan never had any older brother. He pinched me in the buttock secretly so that I wouldn't give him away, and continued.

"You were given that name, undoubtedly, so that you would be a rich, gracious and generous man. Listen, Daulet, we're really in a hurry. Pour us each a *piyala* of *kumys*."

"Mama will yell at me. She said that we were to send it to the aul."

"Send what?"

"The kumys."

"But my dear. Zhumeken himself allowed us to drink a little *kumys*. Go on, bring us the cups."

"Mama will yell at me…"

"She won't yell at you, we will pay you money."

Sultan took several crumpled ruble notes out of his pocket and showed them to the boy. He stared at them as if he couldn't believe they were real.

"Yes, yes, we will pay you," I said, supporting Sultan, deciding that that would be more humane than just deceiving the simple-minded Daulet.

---

[36] A *piyala* is a wide drinking cup or bowl in Central Asia.
[37] The *tor* is the most respected place in the yurt.

"But what if Mama comes, what will I do?"

That meant that Daulet had finally consented.

"She won't come!" said Sultan. "Where would she come from? Let that one," he pointed to me with his finger, "watch through the slit, and you and I will quickly pour the *kumys* into the *piyalas.*

Daulet stretched out his hand.

"Give me the money first."

"Here," said Sultan, and thrust the ruble at Daulet.

"It's torn and old."

"Well, then take this one," said Sultan, and exchanged the worn ruble for the new, crisp bill.

The magic power of money drastically changed the expression on Daulet's face. Now a spark of joy awoke in his eyes, and he looked at us far more welcomingly.

It was hard to follow Sultan's action. With a quick motion imperceptible to the eye, he drew out the hidden *burdyuk* and quickly untied the strings. Daulet brought out from behind a curtain a small blue pan from which it was obvious that *kumys* had been poured before.

"Well now, let's have it!" Sultan raised the *burdyuk* and with one swipe poured a little more than half into the pan.

"That's too much!" yelped Daulet.

"It's nothing terrible," Sultan reassured him.

With the same lightning-quick motion, Sulteken thrust the *burdyuk* into its previous position. Then we each took a *piyala* and scooping it into the pan, greedily set upon the long-awaited drink. Placing the empty pan back behind the curtain, Daulet went up to Sultan.

"Give me another ruble," he said, holding out his hand.

"Why?" said Sultan, not understanding.

"You didn't drink two cups' full, you drank much more."

"Oh, you stupid!" Sultan retorted angrily. "Did we really want to drink so much? We were afraid that your mother would come and you'd get it from her! Out of pity for you, we drank everything there was. It's too bad, of course, that I drank so much. Look at how much my stomach is filled up!"

Not knowing what to say, Daulet silently stood staring at us with wide eyes.

"You had better give us something to eat. I'm getting heart burn from that *kumys*," Sultan told him.

Daulet lowered his outstretched hand and said,

"Will you eat bread?"

"Bring it here. Is there any butter? Bring that, too," Sultan went under the curtain along with Daulet.

"Is that a cooked breast?"

Daulet evidently liked bargaining. He hurried to warn:

"You will also pay for the food!"

Sultan took the left-over breast someone had not finished eating, and, hurriedly biting into it, nodded his head in agreement.

"Alright, we'll pay."

"Pay now."

Sultan gave Daulet another ruble. We buttered the pieces of bread and wolfed them down in satisfaction.

"Well, let's go," said Sultan.

We had just headed toward the door when Daulet blocked my way.

"Want a pen knife?" he asked.

"Show me which?" I said.

Daulet took the knife out of his pants and showed me. It was a typical little cheap pen knife. I didn't like it.

"Do you want a belt?"

"What kind?"

Daulet pulled up his shirt and thrust his dirty tan stomach up to my view, showed me the belt which he had on.

"And what will you do, then? How will you hold your pants up?"

"Don't worry, I will hitch them up with something."

I don't know why, but suddenly I felt sorry for Daulet. And I thought that it would really be mean on our part to rob him down to his belt.

"No, I don't want it, good-bye!"

"Good-bye," replied Daulet with regret.

We quickly jumped on the horse and once again upsetting the dogs, rode on further. The white-chested dog, unrepentant, leapt up high, throwing himself with a hoarse bark at the horses behind, the nimble black bitch nipped at his tail.

Sultan tried to lash at the dog with his whip and sting its muzzle, but the seasoned dog dexterously dodged his blows. It fiercely kept attacking the horse, precisely keeping the distance reachable by the whip. I turned and looked back. Daulet, the little "trader," stood at the door in his pale-blue-and-green cap, his shirt untucked, following us with his long gaze.

CHAPTER NINE

In Which It Is Said What You Will Yourself Will Know Once You Have Read It

"Black Kozhe, look here!"

"Where did you get that?"

"These would make a great *malakhai*[38], don't you think?"

Sultan had in his hands two gray caracul skins.

That was odd. Where did he get those, did they drop from the sky? I reached out my hand and touched them. They were as soft as silk, and impeccably dressed; the outer side of the skins was like a smooth white sheet of paper.

"Hey, where did you get those?"

"The Lord God sent them."

I thought that if the Lord God wanted to give a gift to any mortal, He would likely not have started with Sultan.

"Tell me the truth, where did you get those?"

"Do you like them?"

"They're beautiful!"

"Sulteken does not care where they came from. Mark it well!"

Suddenly, a shepherd appeared before us on a little meadow. He was leading a horse by a halter. Sulteken hurriedly grabbed the caracul skins from my hands and hid them in a leather bag hanging behind his back.

"Mum's the word, Black Kozhe!"

A shadow of suspicion slipped over me. "Did that rascal swipe those skins from that yurt?" I wondered, frightened at the very thought.

The shepherd stood right on the path that we were riding along. Drawing closer, we looked him over. He was a man of medium height with a round face and a small triangular beard. He had a white felt *kalpak*[39], faded from the sun, on his head.

---

[38] A *malakhai* is a fur hat with ear flaps.
[39] A *kalpak* is a high, pointed cap made of wool or felt worn in Central Asia.

"*Salamaleykum*[40], grandfather!"

"*Aleykumsalam*[41]. Do you kids happen to have a light?"

Sultan dug his matches out of his pocket and handed them to the shepherd. It turned out that under the crown of his kalpak he had hidden a ready-made, thick, hand-rolled cigarette. He hurriedly lit it, and, making several greedy drags on it, breathed out in pleasure.

"Oh, how good it is. God grant you health, sonnies! I ran out of matches, curse them, and I've been suffering here for quite a while. What collective farm are you from?"

Sultan elbowed me, and on the fly, made up a lie:

"From Kalinin."

I was surprised. Why was he lying? Why didn't he just name our collective farm, New Life?

We moved further on, and when we had driven a fair distance, I couldn't wait anymore and asked Sultan:

"Hey, why did you say we were from Kalinin? Why did you lie?"

"How stupid you are, Black Kozhe! How do you know, perhaps that's Zhumagul himself, the owner of the yurt, where we just drank the kumys? What if he notices his caracul skins are missing and hurries to find us? Then we won't be there. So let him look for us to his heart's content in far-off Kalinin."

***

The first brigade in which my mother worked as a milk-maid was situated behind a mountain crevice in a little village called Kabana, at the entrance to which was a wide gorge overgrown with virgin pine.

From the side it could seem as if an entire aul was spread out here – several white yurts were visible along with grass huts and tents which made up a little settlement. Not far from the homes was a cattle yard fenced off with a log pen. At the center of the village was a trailer in which likely the office was located. There was a red flag on the roof, the walls were covered with slogans and posters (as I learned later, the trailer was simultaneously the office and the Red Corner[42] of the brigade.)

There was a three-wheel motorcycle parked in front of one of the tents pitched near the river. My heart shuddered. "That's likely that awful Karatay who has come. It looks like his vehicle at that big tent," I thought.

I wasn't wrong. Next to the tent was my mother, fussing around a samovar. When she saw us, she froze in place in surprise.

"Greetings, auntie Millat!" Sultan cried loudly, riding closer. "Your son couldn't get himself a horse, and it's too far to go on foot, so I brought him along with me."

---

[40] *Salamaleykum* is the Kazakh form of the Muslim greeting "Peace be with you."

[41] *Aleykumsalam* is the Kazakh form of the Muslim response to the greeting "Peace be with you," which is "And Peace to you."

[42] The Red Corner was a Soviet institution found in many offices, enterprises and schools. It was a room or corner set aside with a library of Communist books and pamphlets for workers' education.

I immediately recognized the motorcycle which stood by the entrance. It was Karatay's motorcycle. Inside the tent, someone's feet in enormous canvas boots could be glimpsed. Without a doubt, the owner of these feet was Karatay himself. Hearing our voices, he immediately picked up his feet.

"What, he didn't go to camp?" he asked my mother coldly.

"No."

I felt that she wasn't happy with our unexpected arrival. It seemed that Sultan also picked up her mood and didn't start climbing down from the horse.

"I'll come tomorrow and try to find you a horse," he said.

"Alright."

"I see you have finally found yourself a comrade. You're in for some trouble with him."

"I know what to do," I replied.

"I see that."

I went into the tent. Karatay was laying on the *tor*, resting on his cheek. Most likely he was working somewhere nearby, and catching a moment, hurried here. He was wearing a ragged old pair of overalls, covered in oil spots. But his beard, which usually stuck out in all directions in disorder, was this time neatly combed. Karatay rose and then sat with his legs crossed under him. Scratching the back of his head from habit and barely restraining a smile, he spoke to me welcomingly and warmly, trying to get me to like him.

"What, have you come to have a vacation at the *jaylyau*? That was the right thing to do. There's plenty of *kumys* here, fresh air, what's not in abundance?"

Soon, the three of us sat down to tea. After tea, my mother began to get ready to go milking. Karatay bid us farewell and set off. I watched his motorcycle as it raced along the dirt road, crushing the bright green grass and leaving behind a dirty black trail and thought, "Why does he come visit us all the time? What does he need? After all, Mama will never marry him. And if she does…"

That thought instilled horror in me. I chased it away and tried not to think about it. Be gone! Be gone, nasty thoughts! Better that I think of Zhanar, who was left far beyond this mountain. Zhanar. I remember how you confusedly started all around when I called you, "Zhanar!" Maybe I should write her a letter and tell her how I had made my way to the *jaylyau*? Karatay…phew, he was always getting back into my head, no matter what I thought about. Wait, you see, I won't think about you at all. I won't think about you for a moment, even if I pop!

CHAPTER TEN

In Which It Is Told How If You Associate with Good People You Will Achieve Your Dream and If You Associate with Bad People You Will Not Avoid Trouble

The author of this book did not for a moment forget that his first prose work he is writing in the form of a tale. Therefore, he is not dwelling on many insignificant everyday details which every person encounters every day in his life. Otherwise this work would turn not into a short tale, but an enormous novel under the weight of which the shelf of any book store would bend. But for good reason it is said: "The cobbler should stick to his last!" How could we write a novel? For that, above all, we would need many piles of paper, and at least a whole bottle of ink. Furthermore, we would have to sit deadly still on the chair and sit behind the desk for many long months and even years. Who would then go to school and do homework? Who would look for the lost calf? Oh, no, at my age, writing a novel was too hard a job.

But that is all by the way. And now I will return to my tale. From the day that Sultan and I ended up at the *jaylyau*, strange as it may seem, a month had passed. Imagine, a whole month! And it passed as if one day. Because we spent it very happily and interestingly. And it was all thanks to Sulteken. In that entire time, I was not without a horse for a single day. What horses he found me! Put on the saddle, he would say, and away we go! And I would follow him. I didn't ask him where we were going. And why? After all, thanks to Sultan, I could ride horses as much as I wanted to and happily spend my time.

Once, a large *toy*[43] was organized on the *jaylyau*, devoted to Shepherd's Day. Who could remain indifferent to such an event? Sultan and I didn't remain uninvolved. Barely had the first preparations for the holiday begun when we grew impatient.

---

[43] A *toy* is a kind of Central Asian festival with a feast, entertainment and games.

We couldn't wait for the desired day and even readied horses for ourselves, since we wanted to take part in the *kokpar*[44].

On the morning of the day when the feast was to begin, my mother went away to milk the animals, and I, leaning on my elbow, lay in bed and read *Robinson Crusoe*.

Suddenly, I heard the noise of hooves outside and soon after, the loud voice of Sultan.

"Black Kozhe, are you home?"

"Yes."

Sultan jumped to the ground with a thud and went inside.

"What, you idiot, are you still in bed?" he exclaimed, leaning down toward me and grabbing the book out of my hands. "You've always got some books sticking out of your hands! Throw it away! What, have you forgotten that the *toy* is today?"

"Wait, wait, let me mark the spot where I left off."

"You left off here on this page where there is a drawing of a man with a gun or what the devil it is, page 124. Well, now, get up lively now and get dressed! We're going to the feast."

I think it would be excessive to describe the festival. Because you all know how it usually goes. Nowadays, whatever there is, there's plenty of that satisfaction. Whatever holiday there is, there's a toy. For example, when they are giving a bride away to a husband, there is a *toy*, if a child is born, there's a *toy*, over-fulfilling of the plan – a *toy*; a visit from some foreign dignitary – a *toy*; Artillerist Day, Air Force Day, Steel-Worker Day, Builder's Day, Athlete's Day, Miner's Day and many other unnamed days – and always a *toy*. Thank god, we have no shortage of *toys*.

So, we came to the toy. There were a lot of people gathered for the holiday. There were particularly honored guests from Almaty whose cars (ZILs, ZISes, and *Pobedas*[45]) were parked in a long row. All kinds of Moskviches[46] and three-wheel jalopies like Karatay's I don't even count. Moreover, almost all the shepherds from the neighboring two districts had come, and the holiday was at its peak, so it seemed.

We went up to a small huddle of people crowded together and saw that in the center was a wrestling match. After the next round, the voice of one of the hosts of the *toy* rang out:

"Now, the children will perform. Let us start the children's wrestling competition."

Watching the adult wrestlers, I felt how I was seized with an impatient athletic zeal. No sooner had the call for children rung out that I immediately jumped into the center.

"I'll fight!" I said to the host.

---

[44] *Kokpar* is a game like polo, only played with a dead goat's head.
[45] Types of Soviet-era cars, named for the acronyms of their plants. ZIL is for Likhachev Plant, Zavod imenno Likhacheva; ZIS is for the earlier name of this factory, Stalin Plant, *Zavod imenno Stalina*. *Pobeda* is the Russian word for "victory."
[46] The Moskvich is a Soviet-era car.

"Well then, come here. I see you're a lad who is on fire!" he praised me and approvingly clapped me on the back.

The wrestling was between representatives of the two districts. Therefore the host of the feast turned with an invitation to the opposite side:

"Uygursky District, enter your fighter!"

There was a slight bustle among the ranks of the people from Uygursky District and a very dark, hook-nosed boy, even darker than me, stepped out. He had barely separated from his fans when behind my back, there were some outraged voices:

"Hey, is that really a child, he's a real *jigit*!"

"Why are you putting out that giant against this boy?"

"Let's have an appropriate rival!"

"That's unfair!"

However, reddened and inflamed with a zeal for the fight, the host didn't think of heeding this noise.

"Strength against strength! Go!" he cried and pushed me together with the hook-nosed guy.

I knew I had a good undercut and so in the first few minutes, I tried to use this favorite method. To my great chagrin, the long legs of my rival were splayed far apart, and no matter how much I stretched, I couldn't reach them.

Guessing my intentions, the hook-nose spread his legs even further and with all his body fell on me. I pushed him first from one, side then the other, but he didn't even budge from his spot. It seemed that my rival was counting only on the strength of his hands and waiting for the right moment when he could pick me up and throw me on my back. A few times he managed some throws, but each time I landed on his legs, splayed out like a frog's.

Suddenly I thought of one more clever move. I stealthily moved towards a small depression in the ground and falling on my side, with a movement barely visible to the eye, threw the hook-nose over my head. Evidently he hadn't expected this, and flying over me, flopped to the ground. I immediately jumped to my feet, and, not letting the enemy come to his senses, sat down on top of him. The crowd went wild. My fans shouted happily, yelling and congratulating me with victory.

"Good guy!"

"There's a *jigit* like a *jigit*!"

"You will have a long life!"

The host came up and shook my hand and gave me the prize, a two-volume set of the works of the Soviet children's writer, Arkady Gaidar.

I felt my grin split wide to my ears and joy filled my soul. Happily I headed to my previous spot. The loud voice of the host behind my back was calling new wrestlers. Suddenly to my side, out of a thicket of people some man in a bright felt *kalpak* hurried in my direction. I didn't ascribe any particular attention to this and kept on walker further when suddenly he caught up with me, grabbed my arm above the elbow and shouted:

"There you are, you fraudster! Busted!"

Without explaining anything, he dragged me behind him as if I were a tumbleweed. It seemed that I had seen that face somewhere, but I couldn't remember where.

"What…what do you want from me?" I mumbled in fright.

The man dragged me from the crowd and stopped. From the anger boiling in him, his triangular little beard shook slightly.

The stranger grabbed me by my pecs, almost suffocating me and shook me hard.

"I should wring your neck!" he said through gritted teeth. "It's not enough that you deceived my son, drinking and splashing the kumys, you also stole my caraculs!"

I jerked as if a frog had jumped on my back. Now I recognized the man with the bright, blazing eyes. It was the very same shepherd we had met on the road from the *jaylyau* who had asked for a light.

"*Aksakal*,[47] I did not take your caraculs!" I wailed pathetically.

"Then who took them, do you think?"

I wanted to get out of this shameful situation as far as I could, so I honestly confessed.

"The boy who was with me took them."

"Where is he? Whose son is he?" the beard older man asked me ominously.

"He's called Sultan…He's there…he's standing over there."

I led the older man to the place where I had been standing with Sultan. But his trail had gone cold.

"Well?! Where is he?"

"He was just here…"

Drawn by the noise, curious onlookers began to gather around us.

"What happened?"

"Where?"

"What has this boy gotten up to?" they asked each other, forgetting about the fight.

It's true what they say, that shame is stronger than death. I didn't know what to do and was ready to fall through the earth from shame.

"Sultan! Hey, Sultan!" I cried helplessly, looking around.

"There he is, Sultan! He's climbing on a horse and is planning to get away!" somebody's voice ran out.

"I turned around sharply and looking toward the side he was pointing, I saw that Sultan had already jumped on a horse.

"Sultan!" I cried desperately, but he didn't even look at me and lashing the horse with the hip, hurried down the mountain incline.

---

[47] *Aksakal*, lit. "white beard," is a term of respect for an older person.

"He got away! You see, he got away!" I told the older man.

"Eh!" was all he could say in helpless anger.

* * *

You most likely understand yourself what kind of state I was in after the incident I've described. My mother was at that toy. Fortunately, she didn't see what shame her only son had to endure before the eyes of an enormous crowd. Mama was then at another place, where there were performances by artists.

I was depressed as I had ever been in my life. The toy was somewhere off to the side behind me, and I, creeping like a little thief, reached my horse and set off behind Sultan.

I was ready to beat Sultan on the spot if he came into sight. How could I not be angered at this nasty trick! To commit evil with his own hands and not answer for it – what could be more dishonest in a man? I didn't know that Sultan had that sort of cowardly and petty little soul.

"If you associate with a good person, your dreams will be achieved. If you associate with a bad person, you won't avoid trouble," the Kazakhs say, and as you can see, for good reason.

After a little while I made my way to the aul where the horses were kept. But there was no sign of Sultan there. I headed to the farm, but here, too, there was utter silence. All the people were at the festival. I tied up the horse to the pole, went into the tent and stretched out on the bedding. Oh, life, life! What an interesting thing you are...Now you force me to have fun and laugh, now you turn into grief and sorrow! And yet in everything, if you figure it out well, a person himself is to blame!

Asking myself several tormenting questions, I didn't notice how I fell asleep.

"Hey, is anybody here? Come out!" a threatening voice rang out, from which I shuddered and woke up. I jumped outside and saw Sultan's father, the horse-herder Sugur. He was sitting on a large bay horse, with a *kuruk*[48] slung over one hand.

"Where is Sultan?" he asked me threateningly.

"I don't know."

"Why don't you know? Oh you damned rascals! You're two peas in a pod!"

Either because he decided to frighten me, or because in reality he wanted to whip me, he pointed the horse at me and waved his whip. I scuttled backwards and tumbled back into the tent. The bay, angered, banged the tent with her chest and it seemed as she was about to knock it over and crush it under her hooves.

"Take off the saddle and let the horse go!" I heard him cry.

But Sugur himself performed the order he had addressed to me.

---

[48] A *kuruk* is a long wooden stick with a hook to catch horses.

He took off the saddle from the horse tied to the post and pushed it aside, dropping the sweat-cloth in the dust. Then he took the crop and whacking it on the horse's mane, drove him away. Sensing freedom, he neighed happily and playfully cantered off, his tail held high and his hoofs clanging. Sugur headed after him on his own horse at a trot.

For the first time I understood what it mean to "beat a man when he is down." My hurt and anger at Sultan still hadn't settled down and now there had been this encounter. Now I was without a horse. Deciding not to let my mother see it, I brought the saddle into the tent and placed it right up against the wall.

CHAPTER 11

In Which I Tell About My Return to the Aul

That was how unexpectedly my days at the *jaylyau* ended. Without a horse, there was nothing to do, and without a comrade, it was depressing. And here Kozheken in fact lost both one and the other. I tried to go to the farm for a few days, but almost died of boredom. The only thing I could do there was to make up some papers. But the Party organizer, barely reading what I had done, said they wouldn't do at all. "You've written all over this page, and with poetry, even! Is that allowed?!" He sent me to the second brigade. "Now this I understand, is a newspaper! Go and read it for interest. This is how you have to put out Battle Page. Take the example from them!" he told us.

After the Party organizer left, I made a point to head over to the second brigade so as to see the newspaper he praised. I saw that they had done it very simply: they took the newspaper *Sotsialistik Kazakhstan* and completely copied the lead article titled "Let us Raise Cattle-Raising to New Heights." Under the article, there were three names shown from the editorial office and below that, a drawing of a post office box and next to it, a short text: "Comrades, no matter how much we asked, no one has offered us their articles. We await materials from you for our next issue." A little lower, in the corner of the newspaper, I saw a thumb tack. That was it, I was unable to find anything more in that newspaper. In my opinion, our newspaper turned out much more interesting. But of course, my personal opinion, and the opinion of the Party organizer, differed. However, this did not surprise me very much because once I read in a book that in debates, truth is born. I don't remember exactly what book I read that in, so I beg forgiveness of the reader.

One evening, Mama said to me:

"Sonny, don't hang around here with nothing to do, and go back to the aul. Or better, like the other boys, work in the collective farm. You had a vacation – now it's enough."

"Well, I was planning to go back to the aul, anyway," I replied.

The next morning, as luck would have it, a two-ton collective farm truck arrived at the *jaylyau* with feed for the cattle. At the wheel was Kaipzhan, a welcoming and kind-hearted young guy. I got into the cabin next to him and saying good-bye mentally to the *jaylyau*, I headed to the aul.

Like the wind, the truck hurtled along the steppe road, which wound like a dark ribbon through the endless sweet-scented valley and of course the magic dream bird could not sit in his hidden nest. Waving her light wings, with a joyful cry she soared aloft and flew away to the endless far vistas.

Oh, Motherland, home of the Kazakhs! Only a dream can fly from place to place in your expanses! How I love these majestic mountains, this emerald steppe, this translucent river and these quietly sailing white clouds in the blue sky – everything that surrounds me now! Lord, why are you so dear to me, my native land?

I really love nature. I love poetry. No matter how much I read and re-read Abay, over and over I want to read his poetry.

When I hear the *kyui*[49] of Kurmangaza and Dauletkerey, I forget about everything on earth. Paging through the poem of Makhambet, I hear in each word the clatter of thousands of horse hooves, the clang of the sabre and the spike. I bow my head before you, native land! Here were born and lived these great people…

The road along which the truck traveled turned at the mountain crevice, going around Lake Tuzkol and headed toward the aul. This road, of course, was much longer than a straight one would be. However, our "meteor" raced ahead, not letting up on speed, with insatiable greed gobbling kilometer after kilometer. It seemed that now the mountain incline wavered somewhere in the distance ahead, but then it twinkled and remained behind us. A line of telegraph poles making endless ranks along the road, as if chasing each other, ran to meet us. Then close by it seemed, gleaming in the sun, was Lake Tuzkol itself. Our road stretched along its reedy shore now. Just a little ways more – and the lake, slipping somewhere to the side, also fell behind us. Now the road was a straight line directly to the east. The arrow on the speedometers, which had hovered tensely at the same place the entire time suddenly pumped up and crept to "50" and then crossed it and froze, slightly trembling, on the number "60."

Suddenly, Kaipzhan turned the truck, climbed a small hill and went directly on to the dirt.

"*Aga*,[50] where are we going?" I asked in surprise.

"In this gorge, there are guys who are bringing in the hay. We'll pick them up and take them to the aul with us," Kaipzhan replied.

These words did not make me very happy. "Most likely," I thought, "Maykanova is here with them." Yes, and Zhantas as well. I didn't want to see them at all now, and most likely they didn't want to see me, either. The reader of course will recall how our guys headed out to the haying, and I refused and stayed home. I had only to run into Maykanova, and she would undoubtedly immediately start picking on me. But what could I do? After all, it wasn't my truck. Oh, how awful it was not to have my own car!

We pulled up to the foot of the mountain and I saw on the shore of a small noisy creek a bright yurt and a white curtain pulled back. There was a small red flag on the yurt, waving in the wind. A group of young people, sunburnt and looking more like an Indian tribe, ran around the small meadow playing volleyball. We drove in a little more and then came to a stop. The river bed turned out to be rather deep and there were numerous large rocks strewn through it. There was no bridge to be seen across the river. Kaipzhan got out of the truck and coming closer to the shore, shouted loudly:

"Hey, guys! How do we get to the other side?"

Several young boys ran to the river upon hearing the shout. Among them I saw our famous wrestler Batyrbek, who had graduated from seventh grade, and Temir, my fellow classman, chairman of the class council. And over there the annoying Zhantas was running behind him. On his head, he had a home-made pilot's cap made from a newspaper page.

"The crossing is further down! You can't get across here!" the boys shouted.

"If that's the case, pack your things, drag them over here and throw them into the truck!"

It turned out that Batyrbek was the brigadier.

"Duty officer, line up the brigade!" he commanded one of the boys with a red arm band on his naked arm.

The boy ran under the awning, and took into his hands a horn which gleamed in the sun and sounded the notes for line-up and then jumped back outside. No sooner had the horn fallen silent when the boys playing volleyball dropped everything and ran to the awning, quickly lining up in a wide line marked on the ground, and froze. Not believing my eyes, I watched this scene in amazement. Now that's discipline, I understand! Just like in the army.

"Comrade brigadier! All members of the brigade are lined up on the line at your order!" the duty officer reported to Batyrbek.

A minute later, the guys set to taking down and folding up the awning.

I drew myself in, leaning against the back wall of the cabin and tried not to be noticed by any of the guys.

A bitter feeling of regret seized me. "Why didn't I go with them to the hay-making, and went to that idiotic *jaylyau*?" I thought to myself with belated remorse.

The boys brought out a long thick stick from somewhere, hurled it across the river and began to drag things along it.

First to notice me, as I could have expected, was the cunning Zhantas.

"Hey, and where did you come from, you deserter?" he asked mockingly.

"What business is it of yours?" I snarled.

To my good fortune, none of the teachers were there that day. Maykanova had gone to the aul that morning. The luggage was quickly loaded into the truck and the guys, hoisting rucksacks on to their backs and chatting happily, crawled into the back of the truck. Yielding my place in the cabin to the cook-girls, I scrambled into the back with the others.

Slowly turning, the truck wended its way back to the previous road.

Singing songs and shouting, we arrived at the aul. There were several people, including the chairman of the *artel*[51], standing in front of the management office of the collective farm, chatting. The truck drew up and stopped next to them.

"Hello, my dear workers!" Sabyrbayev, the chairman of the artel, joyfully greeted us with outstretched arms and a smile. Next to him stood such scrawny dark-faced *jigit* in a straw hat and a camera around his neck. He differed noticeably from the local residents in his outward appearance, and in the outfit of his craft, he looked like a shorn calf. With our approach, the young man bustled about and said:

"Children, stay in the truck for now!"

I thought if some sort of fellow wanted to photograph us, then please! What, do we spare our noses or something?

At first I stood in the middle of the truck, but then stealthily managed to get to the front and proudly stretched out in front of the camera view. The stranger aimed the camera lens at us and finally took a picture, snapping not just one, but a whole two times.

---

[51] An artel is a cooperative association, which functioned in the Soviet Union until the 1950s.

CHAPTER TWELVE

In Which We Talk About How the Verse 'Zhanar, I Miss You' Appeared in the World

During the whole trip, my thoughts were about Zhanar. I had the feeling that I hadn't seen her for a very long time, although only a month had passed. Where was she now, I wonder? Was she sitting home or had she gone this time to the camp?

I got out of the truck and deliberately made a hook so as to pass by the street where Zhanar's house was. There it was.

I glanced over the yard, which was thickly overgrown with ivy and goose-foot. On the sharp spikes of the fence, several ravens were perched which were light-heartedly chirping discordantly. It was if the house was frozen. Not a soul was visible. I glanced at the gates – there was no lock. And the fresh flatbreads from the oven laid out by the wall indicated that the dark old lady was somewhere nearby.

"Who are you looking for?" an unpleasant voice rang out.

Turning around sharply, I saw Zhantas and grew flustered.

"What's it to you?" I snapped.

Zhantas slung his heavy rucksack off his shoulder. His brown eyes flashed cunningly from under his pilot's cap, pulled down on his forehead. He licked his lips, dry from the wind, and asked:

"What, did you miss somebody?"

"Who? What are you talking about?" I parried, looking at Zhantas.

Zhantas jokingly waved his finger in front of my face and teasingly replied:

"I know, I know who you're looking out for…"

"Well, go and know to your heart's content."

Oh, how boldly I pronounced these words! I suddenly realized that they could have a quite definite meaning and I was terrified. Even so, this was heroism on my part. "Well, let him think what he likes, he deserves it!" I thought about Zhantas.

As I found out later, Zhanar was not home, she had gone to camp. I felt as if I had been left utterly alone in an unpopulated desert. An enormous yearning settled on my shoulders.

Night fell. Spreading out my poetry notebook, I sat alone in the far room. Several moths circled around the lamp and beat against the window. Come to me, come to me, inspiration! Where are you? Let the feelings, overflowing me, spill out into beautiful poetic lines! For the theme of my verse today is Zhanar. Opening a fresh page, I wrote the lines, "Zhanar, I miss you," in the middle with pretty letters.

The first four lines had resounded within me since that very morning and now they easily lay on the paper:

>Zhanar, I miss you!
>Come back, come back quick!
>All these days all thoughts are about you!
>There is no peace in my soul.

I re-read these lines a few times and decided that they had turned out not too bad. Maybe they were weak in the artistic sense, however the truth of real feeling was hidden in them. Either because a pen had long not been in my hand, and therefore my chest heaved the accumulated verses or the feelings bubbling up in me splashed outside, caused by my yearning for Zhanar, but in one stroke, without any difficulty, I wrote poems for a whole two pages.

I think the last stanza was particularly successful:

>Zhanar, there is no other
>And if there is, she's not the one
>Only to you goes my greeting
>My yearning is only for you.

Oh, how great it is to successfully complete something you've started! In the greatest of moods I got up from my seat and looked at the clock. It was almost 11:00 o'clock. It was time to go to bed. I went outside and then returned and lay down in my bed. But can you really fall asleep in such a state? My thoughts were once against occupied with Zhanar. "Braggart Kozha. Now I'll call you Braggart Kozha." I recalled how Zhanar pronounced these words, happily clapping her hands and circling around the room. The verses I had just written about her came to mind. They were just on the tip of my tongue. So that meant I had memorized them. Lying on my back I the total darkness, I began to soundlessly recite them, as if unreeling before my eyes the scenes of a silent movie.

>Zhanar, I miss you...

I reached the last four lines, repeated then – and then suddenly, it was as if an electric shock had hit me. "Stop!" I said to myself. "I think these aren't your verses. But whose are they? Think hard." I thought. My memory feverishly sought the answer to this question. And suddenly my eyes grew round and my breath ragged. So that's it! My God, these are Abay's poetry! Yes, yes, the very ones that start with the words, "Greetings to you, dark-browed!"

The thought that you could become a poet by stealing poetic lines first from one and then another had never occurred to me in a dream or in reality. It seemed horrible to me. What had I done! That's real robbery. Not ordinary robbery, of course, but literary. It even has a special name. Some sort of term...I couldn't remember...

I jumped up from the bed and wanted already to cross out the lines I had borrowed from Abay-*ata*,[52] but then thought better of it. If I do that, first, I will smear the notebook. Secondly, Abay is a great *akyn*[53]. What if a young, beginning poet like me used a few of his verses for good cause? Would his glory diminish or his legacy be less?

I wasn't intending to send them to a publishing house. And therefore it was not worth destroying them, let them stay. In the end, who was Abay and who was I? We were both Kazakhs and both poets. Nowhere was it written that a poet could not help another poet.

---

[52] *Ata* means grandfather, and also a term of respect for an older man.
[53] *Akyn* is an improvising singer.

CHAPTER THIRTEEN

Which Could Be Called 'The Brown Calf'

The beginning of the school year was approaching. This year, I would be going into sixth grade. Before the end of middle school remained another four, no, not four, but five years. Oh, how long it was! If you think hard, it was not so easy to become a human being.

I had already prepared all the necessary textbooks. Mama had given Kaipzhan money so that when he went to Almaty, he could bring back a new, crisp uniform for me. If everything went well, then on the first of September, Kozheken would pass through the streets of the aul in it.

I impatiently waited for the beginning of the school classes. A person is constructed in an interesting way, anyway. When you're studying, you dream of vacation. And now that I was on vacation, I missed school. During the summer, you want winter, and during the winter, you want summer. Why is it that way, eh? Can you ever really please a person?

But I had a fairly good reason to miss school. For me, the beginning of the school year meant that I would be near Zhanar. In fact, I almost forgot. Today was the closing of the season at camp, where she was on vacation. That meant she would be returning home. Hurrah! Zhanar was coming back, Zhanar was coming back!

"Kozhatay, are you home?"

When I'm in a good mood, I'm not at all opposed to kidding with my grandma.

"Maybe I am! Go and look," I replied playfully like a girl.

"If you're home, go and look for the brown calf and drive him to the yard. He won't graze in any event in this heat."

"And if I'm not at home?"

"Go there anyway," Grandmother told me abruptly. But I sometimes like to test her patience.

"How can I go if I'm not home? For I didn't hear what you said?"

"Oh, you blabber-mouth, that's enough nonsense! You heard me. Go means go."

"And if I don't go, *azhe*?[54] What will happen?"

"If you don't go, you'll get it from me!"

"How, cooked or raw?"

Tired of my blabbering, *azhe* fell silent.

Coming out of the house, I slowly headed toward the place where the calves pastured. It was humid, without the slightest wind. The back of my head soon began to burn as if the tip of a sun ray had stuck to it. From time to time, I covered it and stroked it with my hand, feeling my burning and coarse hair, like a pig's bristle.

Soon I was at the edge of the village. On the road, a truck appeared kicking up dust with its wheels and quickly approaching me. The back was filled with children. Their red neckties fluttered in the wind and their cheerful songs could be heard. In the next minute I noticed that it was all our guys returning from camp. Among the girls sat Zhanar. The wind was fluffing her bangs above her forehead, and she was smiling, looking at me. I joyfully waved both hands.

"Hi, Kozha!"

"Hey, Black Kozhe!"

"Kozha!" the voices carried to me from the truck which immediately flew past me.

I was happy that at least for a moment, I could see Zhanar. I really wanted to run after the truck, but I held myself back. At that moment, behind a hillock I saw our brown calf, lazily mooing. Shouting loudly, I spooked him and unexpectedly I found myself chasing it along the road. I hurried along, not feeling my legs beneath me, like a whirlwind from out of nowhere, circling the calf and returning to him, running first on one side of him, then the other. The frightened calf, not realizing what was happening, was galloping along and when he reached the outermost house, crashed into someone else's yard.

Soon I came back on the road, my head spinning from the unexpected chase after the animal. Then I had an idea. If our brown calf could understand human language, I would hug him around the neck, kneel before him and beg him: "My dear calf, I will chase you once again along the road, and you run into Zhanar's yard, please. I will come after you. The dog barks loudly there, and Zhanar will run out of the house. I will tell her something, and she will answer me with something. For I haven't seen her a whole month! That way I can at least see her a little bit and talk to her."

[54] *Azhe* means grandmother.

But how could the brown calf understand me! All I had to do was let him go, and he would immediately be ready to rush home. No, you'll have to wait for your own home. First, you have to serve me. I led the calf to Zhanar's house. Looking all around, I assured myself that no one saw me. It was quiet in the yard. I pushed the calf through the open gate, but he wouldn't budge, reluctant to go into a strange yard. I picked up a thin branch off the ground and whipped the calf a few times hard. On the way, he hit a pail with his hoof, which clattered noisily to the ground. The noise spooked the dog who started up a loud, desperate bark. Just as I had supposed, the door to the house opened and Zhanar ran out on the porch. It turned out that flustered, a person can't say anything smart.

"Zhanar, chase that calf over here, please," I said, not finding any other words. Looking sideways warily at the dog, the calf reached the fence. I led him out of the yard and silently drove him home.

CHAPTER FOURTEEN

In Which It is Told How the Entire Republic Learns About Me

"Hey, is anybody home?"

This was the voice of the postman, the old man Koshtibay.

"Yes!" I said, running outside.

Every year, I surprised to several newspapers and journals. If you like, I can list them: the magazine *Pionir (Pioneer)*; the newspapers *Kazakhstan Pioneri, Pionerskaya Pravda* [Pioneer's Truth], *Leninshil Zhas* Mama took the journal *Kazakhstan Ayelderi*. At first, I regarded this journal with disdain, considering to be strictly a woman's journal. But as it turned out, it was the most interesting.

Koshtibay handed me the journal *Kazakhstan Ayelderi* and *Kazakhstan Pioneri*.

"And there aren't any more?"

"No."

I sat down on the bench near the house and set to reading the newspaper first. Usually, I start reading it from the last page (I think other people do this as well). Because it is there that the most interesting stories are printed, the feuilletons and satirical verses. Then I go to the third, and then the second pages, and with each page, the content of the newspaper becomes less interesting. And as for what is on the first page, I learn about that only from the headlines of the articles.

This fact, I think, tells us that the respected uncles who put out the newspaper don't take the opinion of their reader into account at all. And that's too bad. How wonderful it would be if they put the materials from the last pages on the first page, and the first page on the last. Then you wouldn't have to trouble yourself to read the paper backwards. I tarried a bit on the fourth page of the *Kazakhstan Pioneri*. There was a story printed by a famous children's author, S.S., called "Renewed Streets." Judging from the title and the illustrations, it was about how children had planted green saplings all along a street. Well, that's an important and necessary topic. I even have a poem in that regard, which is called "Let Us

Beautify Our Street."

There were several more satirical poems on that page, some riddles and humorous drawings from the life of the Chinese people.

Turning over the page, I looked at the third page and immediately saw a snapshot placed at the top. It caused a very pleasant impression on me. It showed part of a house with a high roof, a truck, and in the back were a lot of kids with smiling faces and forks and rakes in their hands. I quickly ran my eyes over the credit under the photograph and then like a madman, jumped from my seat and flew into the living room, where *azhe* was sitting.

"*Azhe, azhe!*"

"What, sonny?"

"Look, they printed my photograph in the paper! Look, there I am standing in the middle. See?

Squinting, *azhe* peered at the photograph.

"Which one? I see a whole crowd of people."

"Here…Here I am, in the very middle, see, how proud? That's me."

"And who are the rest?"

"Our guys. Here's Temir, here's Batyrbek with the rakes in his hands, and this one peeking out from behind is Zhantas…See what they write: "Students of the seven-year school of the New Life Collective Farm provided significant help during the summer holidays to the agricultural artel. In the photograph: a group of students who were distinguished by shock-work in the hot toil of the haying…"

Reaching the end of the phrase, I almost bit my tongue. It was good that I read this caption softly, perhaps *azhe* didn't realize what was written here. Tip-toeing away, I slipped out of the house.

How do you like that! And without realizing what was going on, I started bragging. How embarrassing! How everything came out bad! When did I ever take part in the haying? When did I ever do any shock-work?

The gnawing of my conscience bothered me. And once again I remembered the popular wisdom that said that shame was stronger than death. Yes, truly was it said. I glanced at the photograph once again. Everything was just as it had been before in the front row, in the very center, as if I were a hero of labor, proudly, with an imperturbable expression, there was the same Kozha. The upturned nose, the chest thrust out as if to say, look how great I am! What can you say, he vividly stood out from the other kids.

I just had to manage to go and stand in the very center! No, I couldn't find room for myself somewhere off to the side. What devil got into me? Sweat broke out on my brow from worry. Now Zhantas would be first to raise me up to ridicule.

Suddenly, I brightened. Hurrah! I found a way out! I will take some ink and cross out the caption nice and hard so that no one can read it. Then I can boldly run through the aul and show the paper to everyone. But foo, what sort of fool am I?! Did that newspaper really only come out in one copy? Likely many of the kids were reading it now, just like I was...

In a word, that photograph really ruined my mood. But gradually I calmed now and decided not to be depressed. In the end, now, thumping myself in the chest, I could boldly declare to anyone, "Just try and say that I didn't work this summer at the collective farm! What, you can't? But that's it! The newspaper itself is witness to the fact that I took part in the haying!"

CHAPTER FIFTEEN

In Which It is Told How Once I Gave Zhantas a Kick

Today is the first of September. Like a soldier on parade, I dressed up in my new uniform and stepped off to school. I had a new yellow satchel in my hand and on my neck a bright red necktie. That morning, I twirled in front of the mirror for a long time, trying to put my cap on better. Finally, I put it on, slightly tilted to the right. I walked along the street and looked sideways at my shadow. My shadow was long and stretched out and followed me without fail. One of its legs was for some reason a little shorter than the other. And its cap sat on its head wrong, somehow. The crown stuck up on my head quite awkwardly.

Ahead was Zhanar's house. My heart started beating, hammering in my chest. Had Zhanar left for school or not? Walking past her house, I straightened and walked in step, as if it was a government podium. How did I know, perhaps Zhanar was standing at the window right now and looking out at the street? I snuck a glance at the windows. They were empty.

A girl in a white dress with a folder under her arm came out across the neighboring lane. This was Maykanova. I grew flustered at the unexpected encounter. If only it were the end, and not the beginning of the school year, I could pretend I hadn't noticed her and pass by. I jerked my cap from my head and greeted her.

"Greetings, *tatay*[55]!"

"Well, now, Kadyrov, did you have a nice vacation?

My heart sank. I thought she might start up a conversation about Sultan's and my bad deed.

"N-n-not bad," I stuttered.

"Where did you go this summer?"

"To the *jaylyau*."

---

[55] *Tatay* is a term of address for an adult.

"So I thought. You got a deep tan," Maykanova smiled. "Now you really are Black Kozha."[56]

"Oof!" I signed in relief. It seemed Maykanova didn't suspect anything.

I walked alongside her and noticed that I had grown much taller over the summer. Now we were almost the same height. Or perhaps she had become shorter? No, that couldn't be. On the contrary, today she was wearing high heels. Maykanova went along, mincing her slender but not very delicate legs, and her light dress streamed out and then stuck to her with each step.

I went into the school. From the first grade, I had studied within its walls and it was dear and close to my heart. It seemed that the brilliant, freshly-polished floor and the sparkling-clean windows hospitably and joyfully smiled. Here was our classroom. It was empty. Likely I was the first to come. I stood and thought about where I should take a cease for myself. What if I sat opposite the teacher? No, better yet, I suppose, was to sit at the back desk. If the lesson was boring, you could open up the desk top and read some book or write some poetry. Although, although it was known that the worst, failing students sat in the back. Those who were confident of themselves usually sat with importance in the first rows.

What, was I worse than they? So I decided to sit in the first row, face to face with the teacher.

Now I waited impatiently for the arrival of Zhantas (foo, how that name slipped off my tongue?) I mean Zhanar. I wanted to propose to her to sit next to me and then for the whole year we would sit side by side.

One after another, the children came into the class, noisily greeting each other. Zhanar still wasn't there. Hearing the voices of girls behind the door I thought she was coming, but each time, I was disappointed.

Zhantas came into the classroom and slammed the door. He also had on a new school uniform. He came in with such an important step, as if to say, "You see how I am today?" Zhantas saw me, raised his had, and announced loudly:

"Greetings, hero of labor!"

That was what he had nicknamed me ever since the day that our photograph had appeared in the newspaper Kazakhstan Pioneri.

"Is this taken, Black Kozhe?" he said, pointing to the seat next to me.

"I'm saving it for you," I replied snidely.

"Thanks for your concern!" said Zhantas, bowing, and headed to the desk.

I quickly slid to the edge and didn't allow him to sit down.

"It's taken!"

---

56 Here the teacher is referencing the Russian word *kozha* which means "skin," although usually the boy's nickname is "Black Kozhe" for *kozhe* which means millet soup, made from the black grain millet.

"Who's sitting here?"

"What, don't you understand Kazakh? I said clearly: it's taken!"

"What, are you saving it for Zhanar?"

Here, dear reader, blame if you like, don't blame me if you like, but I couldn't take it any more. In the course of one minute, the poisonous tongue of Zhantas had offended me three times. First, Zhantas had mockingly called me a "hero of labor," then deliberately distorted my name, and if that was not enough, he brought in Zhanar's name. I was seized with such a fury that I jumped from my seat, grabbed Zhantas by the shoulders and turning him around sharply, gave him a strong kick in the butt.

No, no matter what you say, Zhantas wasn't a man. If somebody did something like that to me, I would die, but I would pay back for such humiliation. I expected the same in reply from Zhantas and was ready to tear apart the joker. However, in spite of my expectations, Zhantas behaved differently. After falling silent for a while, he only muttered:

"I was just joking…" Even so, the poor guy's joke sounded somehow unsure and pathetic. I didn't hear any force or anger in it.

At that moment, into the classroom walked Zhanar. On her head was my favorite red beret. Caught off guard, I couldn't even say hello. Zhanar walked past me and sat down at a desk somewhere in the center of the classroom.

Once again it was that mean Zhantas. After all, due to him, my well-thought plan had collapsed.

CHAPTER SIXTEEN

In Which Once Again I Meet Sultan and Become Friends, About Fishing on the River Karas. This Chapter Ends With An Oath

I had not seen Sultan since I had returned from the jaylyau. I don't know where he went to all that time. He made himself at home anywhere. He was probably wandering around somewhere, pulling some stunts somewhere as usual.

Oh, Sultan, Sultan! You have so many remarkable abilities that you can only be envied. How you lasso a wild horse with such amazing dexterity! And how wonderfully you know how to whistle, modulating the sound in all sorts of ways! If necessary, you will milk a mare so well that people will be amazed. You are kind and generous. You will give everything away to a friend if need be. But you are also dishonest: you can easily lie. If you had not dropped your studies and you had rid yourself of these qualities, then you would definitely have become a good person.

That was my opinion regarding Sultan. I thought about him fairly often. Ever since that day we had parted, I felt as if I had lost half of myself, as if I was missing something, for when Sulteken was nearby, I didn't notice how the time flew.

Once, when I was returning from school and rounded the corner and was about to go into the yard, a dog of some kind started barking behind me and then grabbed my leg. I yelled at the top of my lungs from the shock and turned around sharply. I look, and there was no dog behind my back. But out from under the bushes, laughing and grabbing his stomach, crawled none other than Sultan.

"Oh, did I scare you but good, Black Kozhe! Hah-hah! You won't find someone more cowardly than you! Go home quick as you can and change your pants! Hah-hah!"

Whatever I might have expected, it wasn't such a happy meeting with Sultan as this, to be honest. I thought that after I betrayed him at the toy, he would want to get his revenge against me and show me where the fish swam. Evidently I was wrong to fear him. Our relations, it seemed, remained as warm and unchanging as before. Sultan was still chuckling cheerfully, holding his stomach. His prank had gone over well. I didn't see a shadow of offense on his face, and not any signs of hostility. Calming down, I quickly took myself in hand and with the look of an offended person, said coldly:

"Get out of here and don't bother me!"

"What happened, Black Kozhe?"

"Why did you leave me that time? What, do you think you did the honest thing?"

"Alright, alright, Black Kozhe. You're still thinking about that? I've already long since squared things with Zhumagul. I gave him a fancy silver cigarette holder…Listen! Do you want to go fishing with me now? Not from the upper crossing of the Kinkbay, but on its other side, I found a great place. It's just swarming with fish, believe it or not. As soon as you get there you pluck them right out.

"Do you have a net?"

"I'll get one from the miller Ivan, he's my friend.

I was not strong enough to resist such an occupation as fishing.

"Alright, but first I'll run and eat."

In the yard, I saw the bay horse that Sultan had manage to tie to a pole before my arrival. I ate hastily and Sultan and I, throwing two saddles on the horse as we had before set off from the yard. Oh, what enjoyment – to ride on horseback! I immediately cheered up, and my heart grew light and happy. On the way, we turned in at the mill. The old miller happily greeted Sultan. They shook each other's hands hard, sat down and had a smoke and spoke animatedly about life and various news.

"Give us your net, please. We want to do a little fishing," Sultan asked after a little while.

"Take it. It's over there on the porch," Ivan said, not hesitating for a moment.

We took the net and went further. Soon we had reached a dense forest and entered it and wove our way along a narrow, half-overgrown path. From time to time, we found some bushes with forest berries. Here and there the slender branches gleamed dully with the bright, red tempting berries. I wanted to jump down and regale myself with them so much that my mouth watered but Sultan didn't like that. He couldn't think about anything except fishing.

The fishing hole that Sultan had spoken about turned out to be in an untouched part of the forest. The water was fairly deep and it was convenient to throw the net from the shore. We tied up the horse further away and stepping carefully on tip-toes, went to the river. I leaned down, stretching my neck and gazed into the water, hoping to see the fish swarming there. Then Sultan kicked the friable shore and in an instant, a whole school of long black fish splashed out of it. They swept up and down and hurriedly swam off in different directions.

"Wow! What a lot of them there are here!" I exclaimed, in spite of myself.

"Shh, don't shout!" Sultan hissed at me.

We quickly undressed and went into the water and began to swim away from the shore. Sultan thrust the net into my hands while he kicked his legs in the water, stirring the soft clay bed with a long stick.

"Raise it!"

I hurriedly tugged the heavy net from the disturbed muddy water and barely hanging on, dragged it to shore and turned it over. The fish slipped downwards into a pile on the grass, slapping each other with their wet tales.

"Hurrah!"

The mouth of the Karasu was nearby, at a small hillock. Again and again, dragging the net, we reached it in about an hour. In the end, there was a whole pile of fish.

And finally, Sultan and I, very satisfied, as if we had been to the most honorable places in paradise, sat down at a little campfire and set about stuffing both cheeks with fried fish, regretting that we didn't have any bread or pans with us. Sultan sat with his cap on backwards and hurriedly sent piece after piece of hot fish burnt on one side into his mouth.

"Black Kozhe, tell me, what's not to like about this life?" he asked, smacking his lips in satisfaction.

Without thinking twice, I said what I thought:

"It's a sweet life!"

"Why do you torture yourself with school? Drop out!"

"Mama would kill me then."

"No way! You think it's so easy to kill a person? Last year my father also said, listen, if you think of dropping out of school, I will skin you alive, and I swear, I'll run off somewhere. But see, he didn't do anything. To be sure, he did give me a licking with his belt on my backside a few times. But in reply to that, I jumped in the river and shouted some curse words, like, 'it's better to drown than live a dog's life.' So his eyes almost popped out of his head from fear. Well, the old man took a fright for real. He chased after me, caught up, and then hugged me hard to himself, begging me, 'if you don't want to go to school, do what you want, as long as you're alive and well.' You should see how all the way home, he kept hugging me and stroking me and kissing me. Ever since that day, my father doesn't even say a peep about school. So if your mother touches you, run right to the police. We don't have a law that parents can beat their children. They can even be punished for that.

Obviously, I was fibbing when I said that my mother would kill me. Perhaps some time in my long-ago childhood she beat her son, I don't know. At any rate, as long as I recall, she didn't lay a finger on me. No matter how mad my mother gets, she either scolded me or silently frowned and that was enough. Only *azhe* could sometimes threaten me,

"Oh, you're going to catch it!" But she never made good on that threat, either.

To be honest, it never occurred to me to leave my studies.

"No, I can't drop out of school!" I said flatly.

"Maybe you're right," Sultan agreed unexpectedly. "What good can come of it if they say that it happened because of me, too. Then we'll both get it! You had better study. Look around, and sooner or later you'll get somewhere. Who knows, perhaps in the future, you might make a big boss. Then at least it will be some use to me. I will come and ask to borrow your car, for example. What, you wouldn't give it to me?"

"I'm not going to be a boss."

"What will you be?"

I had no doubt that I would definitely be a writer when I grew up. But to tell Sultan about this now would be like putting myself up for ridicule.

"I know myself."

Eating our fill, Sultan and I set about cleaning the remaining fish. Evening was approaching, and it was getting noticeably darker in the woods. The mosquitoes descended and a whole swarm whirled around our heads. Sultan gutted the fishes, took out the innards and then fooling around, began slapping himself on the forehead with the fish bladders. Soon his entire forehead was covered in yellow and rose-colored spots.

"Black Kozhe, do you want to become a robber?" he suddenly asked me.

"How?"

"Very simple. We build a grass hut somewhere here in a hidden spot. We dry as much fish as possible. When we want, we'll rob passers-by on the road. In short, we'll live like the real robbers once lived."

"But we don't have anything. No pans or bedding or guns..."

"Nonsense. We'll bring all that here from home," said Sultan. "You know what fun it would be!"

"And what about school?" I said, doubtfully.

"Study as much as you want. We'll only rob at night."

I was intrigued by Sultan's idea. It was so unusual and interesting! One of the nights maybe we could steal Zhanar and bring her into the forest! She could cook us food and do the laundry.

We gutted all the fish and carefully lay it out on branches. Finishing up with this job, we began looking for a good place for our grass hut. We found it not far away, at the very shore, among a thick growth of rose willow. We wove some flexible top branches together, and wound around some stalks, turning them into something like a wall, and it turned out to be a comfortable little nest, with a narrow entry through which only one person could squeeze.

Looking with obvious satisfaction at this little hut, Sultan said:

"Look, Black Kozhe, not bad, eh? Live here a hundred years, and not a soul will find you, unless they accidently stumble on you."

"For sure, they will never find you!" I agreed. Even if somebody did stumble on it, they wouldn't in their lives guess that it was a home.

"Great! This is real life! Let's bring some guns here, I have a great Finnish knife, we'll bring that, too. Oh, Black Kozhe! Wait a little bit, and I'll show you some wonders which you've never dreamed of! Only let's agree right away: the betrayal that happened between us this summer cannot happen again. Let's be honest and devoted friends. A robber is ready to give his life for another robber. So, give me your hand!

We reached out our hands and linked our little fingers. Sultan knocked them on the edge with his left palm.

"Wait, that's not all," he said, and drew a circle on the ground.

"What's that?"

"It's the red hearth. If one of us breaks the oath, he will burn in it, as in hell."

After that, he drew several straight lines across the circle, lay down on his stomach and solemnly touched his forehead at the point of their intersection. I repeated this ritual after him.

CHAPTER SEVENTEEN

In Which is Discussed the Commotion of Feelings Which Fall to the Lot of Every Student

After that crazy day, I slept like the dead. Through sleep I felt *azhe* energetically shaking me by the shoulder.

"Kozha! Kozhatay! My dear, what, you aren't going to school today?"

I opened my eyes and glanced at the wall clock. There was fifteen minutes left before 8:00 a.m. I jumped from the bed as if stung, dressed in a flash, rinsed my face somehow and standing up, splashed some *ayran*[57] into a *piyala* for myself.

The night before, I had barely made my way home from exhaustion and of course didn't prepare a single lesson.

Throwing my textbooks into my satchel, I hurried to school with all my might. Half way there, I heard how the bell rang. My first class was the Russian language. Anfisa Mikhailovna had already opened the door and was on her way into the classroom when she saw me and stopped. Among our teachers, she was truly a golden person. She had come to our school the year before, immediately after graduating from teacher's college, and during the summer had successfully passed her entrance exams, and had entered the institute.

"Kadyrov, what, you overslept?" she smiled and stopped me. "Stop, straighten your tie.

I groped around my shirt and found the ends of my tie on my shoulder. Straightening it, I darted into the classroom. Everyone got up, greeting not me, of course, but the teacher who came in after me. However, I used this in my own way; stopping for a second, I jerked my nose up and gave my face an important expression. Then I placed my hand on my chest and gradually bowed. It seemed like a reply to the greeting. I turned around to see the reaction of Anfisa Mikhailovna – she was smiling, too. Our glances met and she nodded her head as if to say, "Oh, Kadyrov, what you don't cook up!"

---

[57] *Ayran* is a cold salted yoghurt beverage.

She knew how to look into a person's soul.

Don't count me as a braggart, but I was one of the better students in the Russian language. In all the last quarters of the school year, I had had only fives for oral and written answers. Perhaps this was one of the reasons for Anfisa Mikhailovna's good attitude toward me?

The teacher explained our new subject and then turned to the class with a question:

"Well, now children, did you learn by heart the poem by Pushkin, 'Winter's Eve?'"

"*Tate*, may I answer?

"Ask me!"

"Anfisa Mikhailovna, call on me!" the children asked, interrupting each other.

If you knew the state in which Kozheken was in at that moment! For last night, I had not had any opportunity to do my homework. Sultan and I returned home only toward evening. Then he called me to come with him to the pasture, to leave his horse there. Then we decided to find out which of the *jigits* was courting the daughter of Khasen Marzie, and hung around near her house until late in vain.

"Listen, why do we care who is worrying Marzie?" I said to Sultan. "Why do we need to know that?"

"Because we do!" replied Sultan.

"But tell me, why?"

Instead of an answer, Sultan sighed heavily.

"Black Kozhe, you are still too little to understand those things," he muttered a little later.

"Well, understand it yourself then, if that's how it is!" I thought to myself.

As for the poem "Winter's Eve," not only did I not learn it, I had even clean forgot that it had been assigned as homework and recalled it only now, at school. Something twitched at my side from worry. "Horrors! Now that will be a disgrace if I'm called on now!" I thought with fear.

Anfisa Mikhailovna opened her ledger.

"Balabekova!" she called, which was Zhanar's last name.

Could it ever happen that Zhanar would come to class unprepared?

The storm covers the sky with darkness,
Snow blizzards whirling,

She began confidently, and without a snag or a hitch, she recited the whole poem.

"Very good, Balabekova, sit down!"

"Very good!" I praised her mentally myself.

My poor head, now what would it have cost me to copy these ill-fated verses on a paper and take them with me fishing? There, relaxing, I could have easily learned them by heart…

"Tursynbayev!"

Zhantas, who was sitting behind me, dropped the desk top and stood up.

The storm darkness…

"Go to the blackboard!" Anfisa Mikhailovna interrupted him.

"Does it matter?"

Oh, how cunning that Zhantas was! He shouldn't be so deceptive! Apparently he decided to deceive the teacher by keeping one eye on her and the other hidden under his desk top.

But it is not so easy to wind our Anfisa Mikhailovna around your little finger.

Zhantas sniffed and hesitantly headed to the board.

"Well, go on and answer!"

The storm darkness…

Zhantas began softly and then fell silent.

"And?"

"Anfisa Mikhailovna, I didn't manage to learn it…"

"Why?"

"I went to the mill, and I didn't have time…"

Anfisa Mikhailovna looked attentively at Zhantas and said:

"Maybe you can answer from your seat?"

We laughed cheerfully.

"Sit down, Tursynbayev. That is already your second 'two'. Not only did you not prepare your lesson, you wanted to deceive your teacher. You have behaved very badly. Don't let that happen again. Always be honest: if you studied it, you studied it. If you didn't study it, you didn't study it."

That's what you deserve, mean Zhantas! How does it feel to be shamed in front of the whole class? Instead of siccing kids at each other and mocking others, you should do your lessons.

There I sat, laughing at Zhantas, yet at the same time afraid I would be called to the board.

What if she calls on me? What reason will I cite? I will say that I was with Sultan fishing, and getting ready to become a robber?

"Zhakanov, go to the board!"

I signed in relief as if another danger had passed me by. As I have already noticed, each teacher had her manner of calling on pupils. Maykanova, for example, called us in order, sliding her finger down the list from top to bottom. That was frankly very convenient for us. Everyone knew when his turn was coming and was not caught unaware.

Anfisa Mikhailovna behaved differently. First she would call a last name at the beginning of the list, and then go to its end. Some people she called to the board for two days in a row, and others she did not call on for several lessons. In short, no one knew what awaited him at her lessons today or tomorrow.

Now I hoped only for the bell to ring. If only it would ring faster and ease my soul. And for the next lesson, I would study "Winter's Eve" so hard that it would bounce right off my teeth and I would be first to answer.

Now it seemed as if the door of the teachers' room was opening and from there, the teacher on duty was coming out with a nice little bell in her hand. Now, any minute, it would peal out its silver sound.

No, unfortunately, that wasn't the teacher on duty. Lord, the lesson was supposed to end at 45 minutes! Why were they taking so long? Perhaps the teacher on duty had gone out in the yard and got into a conversation with a friend? Oh, it seems like the bell rang. No, I was mistaken again. It was just a cart going by the school and screeching its wheels.

But now Zhakanov had recited the ill-fated verses. And why were they all rattling them off today? The teacher leaned over her ledger, making the next check mark, and I sat there frozen, holding my breath. I wonder who she would call next?

"Kadyrov…"

It was if the sky cracked open above me. I didn't know what to do, I was completely lost. I slowly got up from my seat, feeling the cold sweat break out on my forehead. There are those happy moments that are hard to convey in words! One of them I experienced just at that moment. No sooner did I manage to open my mouth than the cheerful sound of the school bell resounded behind the door. I signed in relief.

"Well, sit down, Kadyrov. I'll ask you next day," said Anfisa Mikhailovna.

My legs weakened and crumpled under me and I plopped down like a sack in my seat.

CHAPTER EIGHTEEN

The Shortest In My Tale

Coming back from school, I saw Sultan. He stood leaning against the fence, gripping a strong whip in his hand. He had folded it in half, and was knocking it against his boot, impatiently waiting for me. "No, I'm not going into the forest today," I decided to myself. "I'll study my lessons. Tomorrow I have to recite 'Winter's Eve' and I have enough homework in my other subjects."

"Drop your books, Black Kozhe, and let's go!"

"No, I'm not going today."

"Why?"

"I'm going to study. I have a lot of homework for tomorrow."

"Oh, Black Kozhe! What are you saying? Come on, let's go, I'll show you something."

We went into the yard. There was a bay horse tied up there. A light hunting rifle hung from the saddle, and both *korzhuns*[58] were packed with potatoes and bread. A black bucket was tied to the straps.

"Here, I've found everything we need. There's also enough ammunition." Sultan drew out of his pocket a whole handful of bullets and showed them to me. "Fifty of them. A friend promised to get me another 100."

I hesitated. Just try not to hesitate, if you see all of that.

"Well, then let's get home earlier. I absolutely must study my lessons."

"Alright, you'll study them."

Soon, riding at a slow pace, we entered the forest on the bay. Sultan sat on the horse, holding the gun for balance, ready to shoot as soon as any rabbit or pheasant appeared. However, except for some clever magpies, we didn't encounter anything. Not seeing anything else, we took turns firing at them, but not a single shot hit the mark.

---

[58] A *korzhun* is a travel bag.

Here was the familiar fishing-hole where we had caught fish the day before. We jumped from the horse and one after another crawled into the grass hut in which we had left yesterday's catch. And then our mouths gaped in surprise. How do you like that?! The branches on which we had laid out the fish to dry were empty. Someone had gobbled them up down to the last little fishy. There were only some fish heads and bones scattered on the ground. Who had done this? Dogs, birds, wolves, or foxes? No matter how much we wracked our brains over these questions, we couldn't think up anything. One thing was clear: it was not a person. First, a person wouldn't start eating raw fish; second, he would likely take the net with him, too. The strange circumstances provoked vague suspicions in us.

We lingered a little more in the grass hut, then undressed and once again threw the net into the water. Surprisingly, the fish that had been here the day before in entire schools had suddenly disappeared. What had happened to them? Perhaps there were less of them? Or they had swum off to another spot? Our labor was in vain – we only managed to catch a few little fishies. However, we still got no less satisfaction from this than from the day before.

If yesterday, we had made do with some fish fried on the campfire without water or salt, today we enjoyed an excellent *ukha*[59] with potatoes.

"How are we going to go on living?" I asked Sultan. "There's no fish."

"We're going to hunt rabbits and pheasants."

"But there aren't any of them, either."

"What do you mean, there aren't any? For your information, this forest is full of rabbits and pheasants. Furthermore, you even find roe deer here. Only you have to hunt for them early in the morning or in the cool of the evening when they come out to feed. In the heat of the day, the roe deer usually lay away somewhere in the undergrowth of the chia or other bushes."

Finally, Sultan and I agreed that the next day – Saturday – we would bring some bedding with us and stay over night here. When twilight came, we would go hunting and at night we would turn into robbers and rob passers-by.

"Agreed?"

"Agreed!"

---

[59] *Ukha* is a kind of fish soup.

CHAPTER NINETEEN

Which Could be Called One Word: "Jealousy"

Maykanova, apparently, had fallen sick because she didn't come to class today. Of course, we weren't terribly upset by this. And could school-children really not rejoice when the class of a disliked teacher was cancelled? There was an incredible amount of noise in the room – everybody was happy at the unexpected break, and then we grabbed a ball and went out to the athletic field to play volleyball. There were two teams in our class which constantly rivaled each other. We ran off to the field and began to play.

If you don't believe me, you can come and see, but I'm not so bad at volleyball. And this time I played with particular inspiration. Catching one after another difficult balls, I deftly knocked them back and tirelessly raced around the field. Perhaps this was also explained by the fact that the girls came to watch our game. How could I play badly if Zhanar came to watch me? Besides, your successful moves and plays make not only your fans happy but you yourself. If you could have seen how I got one of the hardest balls! I jumped to the side after it and managed to hit it back at the last moment over the net, and fell on all fours.

"You go, Black Kozhe!"

"Good guy!"

"Keep it up, Kozha!" I heard from all sides.

I quickly jumped back on my feet and threw a side glance at the girls. They were also happy at my success. But Zhanar…Where was Zhanar? She wasn't there. And I had tried, putting my all into the game, thinking that Zhanar was watching it.

"Eight to eight. Right side's up."

I was supposed to hit the ball. But it was as if some heavy weight fell on my shoulders. With a weakened hand, I hit the ball lazily and it landed on the net.

"Hey, what are you doing, Black Kozhe?"

"What's wrong with you?"

"Where are you looking?"

"Did you miss breakfast or something?"

"It slipped from my hand," I said dismissively.

Our team lost.

"I'm not playing any more," I said and walked off the field, giving my place to another boy.

Where was Zhanar? Maybe she was still in the classroom? She had a custom to sit for a long time behind her desk and read a book. I shook the dust from my hands and headed back into the school. Classes were underway. The door of the 7th grade was ajar, and the voice of Ospanov, the history teacher, could be heard.

"In their effort to acquire equality and preserve their national dignity, the numerically-small people must above all unite. Otherwise, cunning imperialists will not allow them to open their mouths."

I went into the classroom. I entered – and froze in the doorway. It would have been better for me never to have seen what I saw before my eyes. There were two people in the classroom. Zhanar and Zhantas. No one else except them. And they were sitting not just any way, but behind one desk – Zhanar's desk – close to each other, leaning over some magazine. They were so caught up in their reading that they didn't even notice how their heads were touching. They looked up at me briefly, then both turned back to the magazine, which Zhantas was reading aloud.

"What are you reading?" I asked and went up to them. No answer followed. I glanced at the magazine and saw that it was a story about the Czechoslovak travelers Zigmund and Ganzelka, writing about Africa. Zhantas, as if deliberately, was reading in a lively and expressive manner, so Zhanar was listening raptly.

I hung around nearby and didn't know what to do. A hot wave had risen up inside of me. I had never gotten to sit with Zhanar like that, shoulder to shoulder. How stupid I was! I could have thought up the same thing – to bring interesting magazines and read them to Zhanar in between classes. Oh, that cunning Zhantas...

"Let's go play volleyball!" I said, tugging Zhantas by the shoulder.

And here Zhanar suddenly looked at me unhappily and said:

"Kozha, don't bother us!"

How do you like that?! Could I have ever imagined that I would hear something like that from her? I shrank inside myself as if scalded with boiling water and went to my desk, took my satchel and began pointlessly to dig around in it. My heart hammered in my chest so that I thought it would jump out. "What an idiot! What an idiot I am! I can never think up anything smart myself. I'm always envying others' ideas. But will my own head ever understand anything or not?" I said, scolding myself.

I left my satchel in peace and headed to the exit trying not to pay any attention to the two of them. But at the very door, I couldn't stand it any more and glanced sideways at Zhanar. At that very moment, Zhanar was staring at me from under her brow. Our eyes met. It seemed to me that Zhanar's eyes were smiling. What they were smiling at – me or the article – I don't know. At that moment I couldn't care. In response to that smile, I put on a frown and angrily knitting my brows, I left the classroom.

CHAPTER TWENTY

In Which Two Hard-to-Describe Things Are Discussed

No, I had to speak to Zhanar. Perhaps she didn't even guess that I... that I really...Oh, it was hard and terrible to pronounce that word! But no wonder it is said that even if you hide the disease, death will expose it anyway. If I remain silent about this, it will be known in the future. Therefore, it is better to tell my read the truth now. Most likely, Zhanar had not guessed that I was...in love with her. If she knew that, she wouldn't sit with Zhantas like that! Therefore, I had to tell her about all this. About what I will be when I grow up, how Zhanar should not love anyone now but me – in short, about everything – and to come clean. For sure. And today. As soon as the lessons ended I would walk home with her and along the way, say, "Zhanar, forgive me, but I have to tell you something. I'm..." and here I would tell her exactly how it was. Couldn't I do that? I wasn't a coward. I wouldn't budge from my spot if I couldn't do this.

Now the last class was finished. I came out of the school with Zhanar and stepped along with her on the way home. My heart was fluttering. I looked behind me and saw that the cunning Zhantas was behind me. It seemed to me that he was watching me mockingly as if to say why are you slowing down, say what you planned, since you're getting on your high horse. It was as if his gaze had attached to me and kept following me: well, go ahead and say it, if you're so brave! I even shook from agitation, as if not only Zhantas, but all the other kids were watching Zhanar and me and waiting to see what we would talk about.

No, I had better write her a letter. Yes, yes, that will be better, of course. In a conversation, you can leave something out or forget something, but in a letter, I will say everything that is agitating me, I thought.

The weather today was not welcoming. Autumn apparently decided to remind us of its presence. It was cool, and an intermittent wind drew grey clouds over the whole sky. Clear, blue and tranquil, it frowned and threatened to pour rain at any moment. Yellow and crimson leaves scuttled along the streets here and there.

While I was having breakfast, outside the first drops of rain knocked on the window. In a minute they turned into a powerful downpour which beat now first on the windowpane, then on the wall of the house, like a madman.

Through the open door I could smell the sharp odor of dust raised from the earth by the rain.

"Oh, you've gone mad, you bad one!" *azhe* grumbled and hurried to close the door which had flung open. A strong gust of wind, as if in revenge for her words, whipped around her legs at the threshold and blew the wide head of her long dress out like a balloon.

Sultan and I had agreed to meet today, and I waited for him to come any minute. But he didn't come. That actually made me happier than sad. I sat down at the table, placing a clean piece of paper before me, and started to write a letter to Zhanar. The clock showed half-past one.

It was already two o'clock...

Then it was two-thirty...

Three o'clock...

The table was covered with torn and crumpled pieces of paper. These were all my letters to Zhanar. I would write one – and not like it, tear it up and set about writing another. Then that one didn't turn out, and once again I tore it up. I wrote practically a whole notebook full of pages that way. I tried to write both prose and poetry, but each time the tumultuous, hot feelings which overwhelmed me would blink for a moment on paper and then become lifeless.

"Zhanar, I really love you strongly!"

Phew, what stupidity! Can you really love strongly or not strongly?

"Zhanar, I love you!"

Phew, that turned out crude. Just like a movie.

"Zh...Let's be like Kozy and Bayan."

No, that's bad, too. Without any prelude, and immediately taking the bull by the horn. It can't be done that way. At first, it has to be subtle and you have to carefully hint at your subject, and then later gradually develop your thought and explain everything that's necessary. But how, how could I hint and develop?

On the whole, I finally became convinced that it was hardest of all to write two things: a letter to a girl and a tale. It was not like verses. If they were born in you, they so wanted to come out that you barely managed to write them down. Prose was another matter. You encounter so many difficulties here. For example, I've been writing my tale for two or three months already and to this day I don't know how I'm going to end it. No matter what the case, I can't wait to reach its logical conclusion and say, "Well, dear reader, I did what I could, now it's your turn. Be my judge and evaluate my work."

Undoubtedly, if I thought up a tale from my head or wrote about something else, then I would know exactly where it ended. But now I had completely different circumstances. Now I, like a picky inspector, was restoring the chain of events that had occurred in my life. I could write them as they first came to mind, and not torment myself over how to connect one to another and create a united whole. But then can you speak of a full-fledged artistic work then?

Of course not. As the critics say, a writer must select and pick out only what is necessary and valuable, to artistically separate out each crumb of his work and skillfully lay out one after another into a solid, single thread. Does my talent and ability suffice for these niceties of the author's craft? Have I not tired my dear reader? These questions relentlessly persecute, torture and frighten me.

But, my friends, there is no art or high achievements without suffering, after all. As they say, cheapness is for cheap taste. It is not our custom to shrink before difficulties. Therefore, having begun this difficult task – even if I have to sweat and slave – I am bound to finish it.

CHAPTER TWENTY-ONE

In Which the First and Last Day of Our Robbers' Life Will Be Described

The rain which had begun yesterday morning didn't let up until evening, and Sultan and I couldn't get out to the forest. On the next morning, when I awoke, I immediately looked at the sky. It was a clear and shining spotless light blue.

"Let's go!" I said to Sulteken.

"Let's go."

We saddled the bay horse as usual with two saddles, climbed atop the horse and headed toward the forest. We were both armed. On my belt hung Sultan's knife with the bone handle and the hunting rifles dangled at Sultan's saddle. Blessing ourselves and wishing ourselves luck, we went out hunting. By noon, we had wandered through the forest without the slightest result. Twice we had encountered a rabbit, but he disappeared so quickly into the bushes that it was impossible even to take aim at it – or even follow it with your gaze. Even so, hoping for good luck, we fired on it at random and thus wasted a few rounds needlessly.

Frustrated and exhausted, we rode along the river and saw a flock of domesticated geese. The place was deserted and was quite far from the aul. Sultan took up his loaded gun and said to me:

"You want me to shoot one of them?"

"Don't, you'll get in trouble."

But no sooner did I say that than the rifle thundered. One of the geese closer to us waved its wing and fell on its side. It jerked a few times, straightened out its leg stiffly and fell silent.

"Damn! You shouldn't have done that. Now what will we do?"

"Don't worry. No one saw it. Let's take it to our hut, cook it and eat it."

We picked up the goose and hurried to our camp. Once again, we found an unpleasant surprise there. There was total disorder in the hut once again. The sack with provisions which we had tied tightly and hidden in a safe spot was torn and gutted. The unknown thief had eaten all the bread and strewn the potatoes all over.

"I think all of this mischief is from a clever fox," Sultan surmised.

We were really hungry now and without a second thought set about preparing lunch. Sultan began hastily plucking the goose and I gathered kindling and lit a fire.

The goose turned out to be rather large and fat. Sulteken raised it by its long feet over the fire and turning it from side to side, baked it.

Suddenly, right before us out from the nearest trees, emerged a lone man on horseback. Sultan and I didn't even manage to blink an eye, let alone hide the goose. The rider turned out to be the father of our school principal, the old man Akhmet.

"Hey, kids, what are you doing here?" he asked.

"We just…shot a goose. And we want to cook it and eat it," my friend said hesitantly.

"And where did you shoot him down?"

"He flew over our head and we popped him," Sultan said, jerking his head up.

"Your goose doesn't look like a wild one," the old man said doubtfully. "He's awfully big."

"But we especially picked out a fatter one when we aimed," Sultan said, not flustered.

The old man looked at our things strewn about, the pots and pans, and threw a glance at the grass hut, realized this was our favorite spot, and asked with even more suspicion:

"Obviously you've settled in here pretty well, eh?"

"We were fishing," I said.

"And did you happen to catch sight of a hobbled ginger horse?"

"No, we didn't see one."

The old man turned his horse, and leaving us, said,

"Oh, you bad boys, I sense that you've done somebody some real harm. That goose, from all appearances, is not wild at all. And what are you doing hunting wild geese, anyway! Mark my words, if I find out that anybody here is missing a goose, you're going to be in for it!"

I realized that things were bad, and got really scared.

The thought of digging in there in that little spot and being robbers suddenly left us. The encounter with Akhmet foretold us the inevitable end of that plan. Only now we realized what idiots we were, thinking that our refuge two steps away from the aul wouldn't be found by anyone ever, as if it were somewhere on an uninhabited island. And could robbers really survive in our time? They had been in the long-ago past, and had robbed all kinds of bai[60] then. And who were we planning to rob? Nowadays, if you so much as touch anybody with a finger, let alone rob them, the police will be called and in two shakes you'll be thrown behind bars.

---

[60] *Bai* are wealthy landowners.

In short, after brief reflections, Sultan and I came to an entirely definite conclusion regarding our raiding plans.

The goose that Sultan had shot down was really fat and didn't fit in the pail. We had to divide it up and cook it in two stages. We ate it until nightfall, and barely managed to finish. From time to time, we caught fish, went for a swim, picked berries to pass the time, then gathered up the pots, rolled up the net, and headed home. This was the first and last day of our robbers' life.

CHAPTER TWENTY-TWO

In Which is Discussed the Fuss Raised About the Goose and the Frogs, On the Return of Mama from the Jaylyau and How Azhe Defended Me

No wonder they say "Trouble does not walk alone." Within two or three days, so much happened to me that my head spun round. To the fuss about the frog which nearly frightened Maykanova to death was added the scandal with Abdibay. The problem is that the owner of the goose we had shot down was a store merchant named Abdibay. Hearing who had done this, his loud-voiced wife appeared at our house and began to shout to the skies. What didn't she say to us, what words of accusations we heard from this unleashed fury! "Robber! Brigand! Thief! Assassin! If you do such things in childhood, what good will come of you in the future? You'll probably stab someone and end up behind bars!"

Likely, I had known myself poorly up to that moment because when I heard such things, I was horrified. Lord, am I really such a thing?

Soon after his wife came, Abdibay himself came running, out of breath. No wonder people said about him that he was able to shear down from an egg and cut meat from a naked bone. He was a great miser, who wouldn't give you snow in winter.

"That goose was unusual, a rare breed. You won't find another in this district, even throughout this region!" he claimed and finally took in exchange our black lamb.

That, however, seemed insufficient to him, and he dragged me to the principal of the school as well.

Our principal, Akhmetov, was a very strict man. To be honest, each time I ended up before him, my heart shriveled. His cold, penetrating stare from under knitted brows penetrated to your very bones.

Only yesterday I had spent a whole hour languishing in his office thanks to that very frog which almost caused Maykanova to faint, and had left there, half alive. Now not even a day had passed and once again I was standing before the principal with my head hung guiltily.

Abdibay, mixing truth and invention, set about hastily telling the story of the calamity that had occurred to his goose. Akhmetov listened silently, without interrupting him, his face impassive. Only from time to time did he turn on me his penetrating gaze. I was already stubbornly looking at my feet.

After hearing out Abdibay, Akhmetov reached for the telephone, took the receiver and began to dial a number. A second later he was asking someone to connect him to the first brigade of the dairy farm.

"Hello, who's at the telephone?" the director asked a little while later. "Oh, it's you, Millat-*apay*! How are things with you? This is Akhmetov on the line, the school principal. Thank you, everything's fine. Millat-*apay*, I'm calling you regarding this matter: you must return immediately to the aul. There is an emergency. Regarding your son. We plan to discuss this issue at the teacher's council in your presence. I must bring to your attention that your son has taken a very bad road."

My heart shrank as if it had been plunged in boiling oil, even as chills went up my spine. If the earth could have opened up before me at that moment, without a second thought, I would have shut my eyes and thrown myself into the abyss.

Akhmetov still kept talking for a long time to my mother, and finally hung up the phone and said to me:

"When your mother comes back from the *jaylyau*, then we'll talk, but for now, go along."

I don't recall how I left the school. My poor mother, how she must feel now after that conversation! Now she likely couldn't sleep or eat calmly after that conversation. How I had tormented a person who was already not very happy! Last year, Maykanova had buzzed in her ears constantly: Kozha is this, Kozha is that, Kozha has done this, Kozha has done that. And now? Not a month had gone by since the start of the school year, and it was all repeating again...

The roof of our shed was covered with a whole shock of young, sweet-scented clover. Coming into the yard, but not yet going inside the house, I climbed up on the shed, made a little indentation like a burrow and rolled myself into a ball there. I didn't want to see anything or hear anything. All kinds of thoughts came into my head. What would they say at the teachers' council, I wonder? Oh, if only tomorrow would pass favorably! Then I would be quieter than water and lower than grass.

In this difficult hour for me, my friend Sultan, who should have been my bulwark, once again disappeared without a trace. That nasty liar, he had promised to bring the net back to the miller, but there it was, lying on our roof! It turns out you have no humanity in you, Sultan, I thought. Now I'm not going to get near you. Overcome with heavy thoughts, I fell asleep without realizing it.

A sharp crack right over my head forced me to wake up abruptly. I opened my eyes and saw that it was evening already. When I had dug into the clover and fallen asleep, it had been about five o'clock. How long I had been asleep!

The three-wheeled motorcycle stood facing the doorway. Two people got off it – a man and a woman. Recognizing the owner of the motorcycle, I involuntarily shivered. It was Karatay. Next to him stood my mother. *Azhe* came into the yard from the street, carrying a tripod from the kettle.

"Is that you, Millat? How did you get back on your horse?"

In the words of *azhe*, who perfectly saw that Mama and Karatay had come back on the motorcycle and not on a horse, I heard some irony.

"Why are you going around with that tripod?" my mother asked.

"No doubt the children were fooling around and broke one of its legs. I took it to the blacksmith to get it fixed."

"Oh, Lord! Why did you fuss with that? Throw it out, and that's it – we don't even use it."

"Why throw it out? It's something, after all. Moreover, it once belonged to my deceased father. Although it's not much, it's something to remember him by. And did you come back for no reason?"

"Can a person drop their work and come back for no reason? Everything is due to our disruptor here, he can't sit still! He's created a scandal for the whole world!"

"Well, what has he done? Did he rob or kill anybody?" *azhe* said, surprised.

"What, stealing another person's goose and eating it isn't robbery in your view? And scaring the teacher half to death? Such a person could kill anyone!"

"But they told the children themselves in school to bring frogs. Not just Kozha alone – the other boys caught them at the river. They say that the teacher asked them to bring them to dissect at a lesson. And now you see Kozha once again ends up being the one punished."

"But who told him to put the frog in his teacher's briefcase?"

"Do you think he did that? No doubt the croaker crawled in there itself!"

Azhe's words warmed my heart. How she selflessly defended her wayward grandson! Oh, my nice, kind azhe! For you have stood behind me like a wall, knowing full well that in fact I was largely guilty.

"You spoil him too much, you protect him when you shouldn't, and you're only ruining him. If you would just once be more strict with him, he wouldn't be such a hooligan.

"My *Kozhash*[61] – God grant him long years – is no worse than others. When he grows up a little, he will change on his own. After all, he takes after his *nagashi*[62], Sabyrebek. He was like Khozhatay as well – he was a hopeless prankster in childhood. This one at least goes to school and

---

[61] *Kozhash* is an affectionate form of the name Kozha.
[62] *Nagashi* is a maternal relative.

listens to his teachers and only fools around rarely, but at his age, his *nagashi Sabyrebek* got a stick to his head from the mullah and made himself scarce. And when he grew up and had his own little children, he became quite different. The same with my Kozhatay, he will straighten out some day. All children grow up, how can it be otherwise!" said *azhe*.

"Oh, Lord!" my mother said, waving her hand. "Can a child grow up good when he hears things like that?"

CHAPTER TWENTY-THREE

I Suppose the Saddest One in the Book

"Which one of you can catch and bring a frog to class tomorrow?" our zoology teacher Ospanov had asked at the end of the lesson.

"Me!" I cried.

"Alright, Kadyrov. Only look out that you don't forget."

"How many should I bring?"

"One…or no…I suppose two. That's enough."

I had brought in not just one or two, but a whole five frogs which filled the empty tin can which had once held tooth powder. All of them, except for one, were tiny.

The first lesson of the day was the Kazakh language. Coming into the classroom, Maykanova had gone to the desk, placed her ledger there right before my nose, along with her bag, and then went out. The bell had not yet rang for class. And then I had been seized with a devious idea. I had taken one of the frogs and tucked it into Maykanova's bag. Then I had wondered what would happen.

The bell rang, and class had begun. Maykanova had taken attendance according to the list, then had opened her bag and taken out a handkerchief. At that moment, a little gray-green frog had hopped out and jumped right on the teacher's hand. Maykanova had shrieked. Her face grew pale and swaying, she had slowly sat down at her desk…

After that incident, she was not in school for two days. They say she had fallen ill from fright.

Only today did she finally come back to work. The story of the frog was now the talk of the whole school.

…It was getting dark. I kept laying on the roof of the shed in the sweet-smelling bed of clover. What should I do? How could I face my mother? And that Karatay…He was sure stuck on her! He followed her around like a shadow. Was she really planning to marry him? No, that couldn't be.

After a little while, they came out of the house. Karatay started up his motorcycle and turned it to face the street.

"Go away, go away from here faster!" I chased him away mentally. But he didn't leave, and kept talking about something with my mother. It was impossible to tell what they were talking about because of the rumble of the motor. I watched them, and sometimes it started to seem to me that Karatay, talking to my mother, was moving too close to her. "Now stop! Where are you going?" I asked him threateningly, grabbing his collar and roughly turning him around and abruptly throwing him into the street. Karatay flew into the dusty road and lay there like a dead cat. Alas! All of this was only in my imagination, of course.

Finally, Karatay said good-bye to Mama, got on his motorcycle and left. For a time, my mother watched him drive away and then turned around and went inside.

There's a limit to everything on the earth. How long could I lay on the roof of the shed? It was time to climb down. Slipping down on the other side of the shed, I shook the grass off myself and straightened my clothing. My heart was in my mouth from worry. I worked up my courage and headed into the house. I barely managed to pull the door to myself, my heart suddenly sinking. I held my breath. No doubt I looked like an alien from another planet then. Azhe met me in the front room.

"Where have you been? Your mother is waiting for you," she said, pointing to the door of the room. She then whispered, "Watch out, she's very mad at you."

I went into the room. Mama lay on her bed, still dressed, rolled up in a fetal position, her face to the wall.

"Mama!"

No answer followed. I went up to her bed and saw that Mama's hands were pressing a handkerchief to her eyes. It was as if my heart was sliced with a razor.

"Mama, are you crying?"

Mama slowly raised her head and turned toward me. Her brown eyes, full of tears, were cold and alien.

"Yes, I'm crying," she replied with a slightly hoarse voice. "How can such an unhappy one as I not cry? Allah has not given me anything but tears. And you with your pranks will put me in the grave soon. Tell me, please, what goes on with you day after day? What is this nightmare? You're turning into a real hooligan, a dare-devil. How ashamed you should be, in front of people and your friends! You're poisoning your mother's life! Because of you, I can't look anyone in the eye. What can I do with you? What? Why can't you live quietly and calmly? What do you need?"

"Mamochka[63], stop, don't. I'm going to…"

"Don't come near me and don't call me 'Mama'! Better God had left me alone my whole life than torment me with such a son as you."

"Mamochka, stop, please…Forgive me for the last time. I swear…"

I fell at my mother's knees, hugging them tightly, and burying my face in them, began sobbing loudly.

---

[63] *Mamochka* is a diminutive of Mama, to show affection.

CHAPTER TWENTY-FOUR

In Which There is the Teacher's Council

Thus, our round planet turned tirelessly, and from habit, made one more turn on its axis. History aged by one more day. Just think what it brought humankind in those 24 hours! What different events happened to people in that time! How many new people appeared on the earth and how many people left this world, making way for others! During these 24 hours, the light of joy and happiness had been lit in some happy hearts. But how many human souls had been turned to grief and sorrow by pitiless fate? I was in this latter group.

In all my 13 years, this was the most difficult day for me.

It was dark outside. It was quiet all around. Only silly dogs were putting up a senseless whine here and there. All one had to do in one corner of the street was start barking and then another would start. Then one after another, all the dogs in the aul would start barking as if kicking up a row, "What's this? What happened?" In that canine cacophony there was the lazy whine of the old dogs, wizened by life; the thin, penetrating yipping of the young pups; the hoarse, ragged bark of the old hounds; the whining, cutting sound of the young bitches. Oh, dogs, dogs! How many of you have bred, and what breed don't you see among us! When are you going to simply get tired of barking and nipping people in the heels?

Mama and I went to the teachers' council together. Either because the autumn wind was cool or because of worry, I was frozen and slightly shaking.

Somebody was standing at the door of the school and smoking. From the dark silhouette against the dark sky, I recognized Akhmetov. He was in riding-breeches which accentuated his long, thin legs. His greasy straight hair, combed with a straight part, was lifted by a light wind.

"We're expecting you," he said to Mama, and taking her by the hand, immediately led her inside. I was ordered to stay nearby and wait when she would be called.

I climbed up to the porch and sat on a bench there. From somewhere around the corner, someone's shuffling steps and the knock of their cane could be heard. Then the man himself came into view. It was the school guard, old Saybek. Noticing me, Saybek stopped short and like a guard at the border, asked me in a strict voice:

"Who's there?"

"I am, grandfather."

"Who's that?"

"Me, Kozha."

"Why are you sitting here?"

"I came for the teacher's council."

"And what do you have to do with that?"

"My case is being decided there."

"Your case? What case? What, do they want to make you a teacher?"

"No, a principal."

"Oh, that's quite good. Then you'll get a big salary," Saybek said, coming up the stairs next to me. "Eh, Kozha, your late father was a very good man. If you take after him, you will become something more than a principal. But I'm afraid that you don't take after your father."

The old man fell silent and continued:

"'How was it?'" you ask. Here's how it was. In the autumn of that year, when our collective farm was formed, I took a horse from your father and rode it to the mill. I remember that it was a wonderful bay ambler. Times were hard, most people didn't have cattle or horses. So I rode on that wonderful horse to the mill and killed him. And that was only my fault. I had forgot to water the horse, who was tortured with thirst. I hobbled him and let him graze in the meadow. Evidently he sensed some water and headed toward it, but fell in a swamp and drowned. I found him the next morning. Like a duck diving into the water, he went head first into the muck, leaving only the rear of his trunk sticking up. I called 10 *jigits*. We wound the horse around with rope and all of us together dragged him out of the swamp. Any other person in your father's place would have forced me to pay for the loss. But the late Kadyr was a rare human being with a big soul."

"'You didn't want to cause me ill. You see, such a fate was prepared for him!' he uttered without excessive words. Such an intelligent and unselfish man was your father." Saybek thought for a moment and added. "But you...but no, I suppose, not you alone but all school children today, are stupid, in the majority. You ask why? Because when we tell you not to act up and study hard, you do just the opposite!"

Now the door to the teacher's room opened and the voice of Ospanov was heard.

"Kadyrov, where are you? Come here!"

"Run along, they're calling you, you little prankster," the old man Saybek said, clapping me on the back.

I think if there was a pupil in our school who landed in the principal's office the most, that would be me. And here I was again standing in my usual place, where Maykanova had brought me many a time, and where many a time I had given a firm promise to be meek and obedient in the future. But this time I went into the principal's office with particular alarm. I crossed the threshold and stood at the Dutch stove, leaning my back against its cold wall. Akhmetov sat across me at a desk, with his hair combed in a straight part. His face was strict and the straight lines between his brows were deeper and sharper than usual.

"Come closer," he said and pointed to a pen in the center of the room. I made two or three hesitant steps, as if I was before a yawning trap. The gazes of the teachers who sat along both walls penetrated me through with invisible arrows. Maykanova's eyes seemed to stare at me the most hard and fast. She was sitting to the right of the principal.

"Kadyrov, you know why we have summoned you here?" asked Akhmetov.

"Yes," I replied.

"Why?"

"For my lack of discipline."

Restrained laughter could be heard in the office.

"You likely have grown sick of school life, and you don't want to study anymore?" Akhmetov asked me once again.

"I do want to...."

"Then why don't you stop your fooling around?!" the principal shouted, putting a particularly emphasis on the word "why," and thumping his heavy palm on the desk. He jumped up from his seat, forcing not only me but everyone in the room to jerk.

"I won't do it anymore...I'm sorry..."

"How many times have you made such a promise? A hundred?" Maykanova put in.

"I won't fool around anymore...I promise."

If you think about it, for each one of my pranks for which I suffered so, there was an explanation. The goose, for example, as I've already said, was shot by Sultan, not by me. And as for the frog, I hadn't put it in her purse so that she would collapse in a faint. How could I have known that she was such a weak-nerved coward? Honestly, I had never thought of the possible consequences of such a joke. It happens with me sometimes – I do something stupid and then later I am eaten up by remorse.

And although there was no ill will in this, I didn't say a single word in my defense. And was there any need? I completely admitted my guilt and asked only for forgiveness. "I'm sorry and believe me one last time. And if I break my promise again, you can apply any punishment to me."

"No, Kadyrov is incorrigible. He has to be expelled from school," said Maykanova.

* * *

Entirely soaked in sweat from worry, I went out on the porch. Saybek was no longer to be seen. I unbuttoned my shirt, and wiped the sweat from my brow and began to think. "What will they decide? Will I really be kicked out of school? Then what will I do?" I thought.

I wanted to go back and put my ear to the key hole and listen to what the teachers were saying. Of course Maykanova would be for getting rid of me, to kick me out of school as quickly as possible. But what would the rest say? Anfisa Mikhailovna, Ospanov, Daubayev…they all liked me. And hadn't Akhmetov said about me, to a visiting inspector from the district department of education, "And here is our school poet, the future Sabit Mukanov." How could they expel me after all that?

I didn't dare go up to the principal's office. What might happen? What if one of the teachers opened the door suddenly and came out? Thinking about that, I walked around the building and came near the window where the teacher's council was. The ground was steep here and the foundation of the building was particularly high in this place. I could hardly reach the window sill even with my hand stretched. Even though the window was open, the voices of the teachers speaking couldn't be heard clearly and it was very hard to understand them.

At the very wall, next to the window, was the school garden. It had been several years since we had planted these young trees here with our own hands which were now rustling their fluffy crowns. I ducked through one of the gaps in the wooden fence, got into the garden, and like a monkey climbed up the tree nearest to the window. Oh, from here, everything that was going on in that room was perfectly visible; Akhmetov was talking about something. He was waving both his arms and sometimes banging his fist on the table and saying something, turning his head from side to side. If I were looking not at the back of his head, but at his face, I might have guessed what he was saying.

To the left of Akhmetov sat Ospanov, who was leaning his chest against the desk, and furiously writing something. Judging from how he wrote without a break, this was the minutes of the meeting of the teacher's council. It likely said that in a certain year, in a certain month, on a certain day, a certain meeting took place. At this meeting was reviewed the special question of the outrageous behavior of the pupil of the sixth grade, Kadyrov, Kozha. This comrade and that comrade had spoken, and had said thus and so…At the end of the minutes there would be several signatures, then this paper would be attached to the bulging cardboard folder and sent into history. In time, it would be sent into the gold reserves of the archives. Years would fly by, the eras would change, new times would come. And this piece of paper with the minutes devoted to my person would wind up in the hands of one of the literary scholars involved in scholarly research. How endless would his joy be on the occasion of this miraculous discovery! Headlines set in the boldest type would appear, "New Facts from the Life of the Famous Writer Kozha Kadyrov!" Books would be written about me, dissertations would be defended about me on the topics, "Kadyrov Kozha and His Teachers"; "Kadyrov Kozha and Maykanova";

"Kadyrov Kozha and the Story of the Frog"; "Kadyrov Kozha and the Incident of the Goose" and so on and so forth. And these minutes would serve as the reason for the enrichment of the literary brotherhood. Ospanov-*agay*! Try to write the record with as much detail as possible and as accurately as possible. Know that you are providing a great and important service to our history now.

All of these thoughts came to my head much later because at that moment, I was in no mood for trips to the far future. I sat on the branch like a curious raven, and all my attention and thoughts were focused on the window of the principal's office, where the teachers had gathered to decide my fate.

Akhmetov was still continuing to speak about something. Like in a film, I saw his movements and gesticulations, but alas could not hear anything. Once again, he struck his fist on the table. That, of course, could only mean one thing: "Such a hooligan must be kicked out of school!"

Finally, Akhmetov finished speaking and sat down. My mother got up. Oh, my poor dear! And ready to go into fire and water for the sake of her son! She had a look on her face as if she were asking, "My dear people, don't deprive my son of his studies! Forgive him one more time!"

If you knew how sorry I was for my mother! Lord, why was I born such a fidget and a trouble-maker?

Now Maykanova had the floor. Of course, I could guess what she was saying. "Kadyrov must be expelled! Such an unmanageable hooligan has no place in our harmonious collective!" Unexpectedly, everyone present broke out laughing. Even Mama smiled. Why were they laughing?! Anfisa Mikhailovna in particular, was enjoying herself. Her shoulders were shaking from laughter. That meant – fun for the cat, death for the mouse!

Once again, my mother got up. She nodded her head in a sign of agreement and said something briefly, "Well, go ahead, expel him from school! Send him wherever you want. I don't have any strength left to battle that madcap!" I imagined her saying.

The teacher's council ended with that, and everyone began to go their ways. I wanted to get down from the tree as fast as possible and run away, but as bad luck would have it, my shoe got stuck between the branches and I couldn't get it out. I twisted it one way and another and then got mad and…I heard the rip of the sole coming off. Some of the teachers meanwhile were coming out on the porch already. I held my breath, hugged the branch and froze.

Akhmetov and Maykanova separated from the rest and turned in my direction. In a minute, I could see them right underneath me.

"Someday, a real man will come of Kadyrov," said Maykanova.

"Yes, that's a fellow with fire!" Akhmetov chimed in.

Moving away, they continued to say something about me, but I couldn't hear anything more. But the little I heard shook and agitated me. I had considered Maykanova my most evil enemy, and she had told the principal that a real man would come of me! I had just heard that with my own ears! How could that be? It was a mystery…

CHAPTER TWENTY FIVE

In Which the Class Meeting is Discussed

My mother helped to explain the incomprehensible and unexpected mystery for me.

"Sonny, you're wrong to get mad at your class director," she said no sooner had I reached home. "That Maykanova is against you or doesn't like you or persecutes you – these are empty words. If that were all the case, she would never have spoken in your defense at the teacher's meeting and wouldn't have sympathized with you. You should know that it's just the opposite, she loves you. She just doesn't like your pranks and tricks. Keep in mind that people who have experienced in their youth the heavy burden of orphanhood very often become easily wounded, offended and volatile. Every one of your pranks is like a needle that sticks into her sensitive soul and she gets very upset about it and goes about scolding you. A person with such a nature as hers finds it very hard to deal with disobedient pupils. Therefore, you stupid kids have to understand that and respect your teacher."

Mama's words forced me to think. And really, what could Maykanova do with me? Nothing. Most likely she scolded us and got angry because she wanted good for us, and wanted us to grow up to be good people.

Yes, Mama was right, we really were idiots and blockheads.

I had not known that Maykanova had grown up as an orphan. And now that I had found that out, I felt sorry for her. That was why she was so thin and dressed so modestly, apparently that was the reason she went around the whole winter in a thin autumn coat. Only a year ago, Maykanova had finished school and of course had not managed to get a wardrobe. And you, Black Kozhe, are just a fool that you tangled with her. Evidently you have an unripe watermelon in your head instead of a brain. Thus, my opinion of Maykanova gradually began to change to directly the opposite.

"How did the teacher's council end?" you ask me. Don't hurry, dear reader, I will tell you everything myself. The decision of the teacher's council was the following: "The question of Kadyrov's behavior must be discussed at a class meeting. If the students of the sixth grade believe Kadyrov's promise to reform and not make trouble in the future and can vouch for him to the principal, then Kadyrov can be left in the school on a trial period. If they can't vouch for him, then Kadyrov Kozha must be transferred to some other school in the district."

That was the final opinion of the teacher's council. The class meeting took place on Monday, right after lessons. Akhmetov himself attended the meeting. The meeting was opened and chaired by Maykanova. At first she read to the class the decision of the teachers' council and then summoned me to the front and asked me:

"What can you say to your comrades?"

What could I say? I repeated what I had said at the teacher's council: "Forgive me for the last time, if I don't keep my word you can punish me as you will."

After that, the floor was given to the other kids. I knew myself who was for me in the class and who was against me. Even the night before, I had figured what they would say. It pretty much came out that way. The first to speak was the class head, Temir. At first he criticized me, and then in the end expressed confidence that I would definitely reform.

"If we expel Kadyrov from this school, what will we be after that? Could we sitting here not help him at all in any way? Or are we so hard and cruel that we can't sympathize with our comrade?" said Temir. His words were resonant and stirring, just like in a book. "We must reform Kadyrov, and I propose for the last time to declare a strict reprimand and leave him in our school."

After Temir, three or four other students spoke. Their opinion largely reiterated Temir's, as if he had drawn an invisible path for the others, and laid down a certain line.

"Thank God!" I thought, seeing such a turn of events, and signed in relief.

"Does anyone else want to speak?"

"I do!" said Zhantas, raising his hand.

As soon as he got up from his seat, he began a speech as rapid-fire as a machine gun.

"Kadyrov must be expelled from school! He will not fulfill his promise, just like last year, when he swore to everyone. Furthermore, he almost scared Maykanova to death. And what's more he…he…writes letters to the girls…"

His last word seemed to split my heart in two. The entire class, as if they were seeing me for the first time, stared at me in incomprehension. I didn't know what to do, and stood there, burning from shame.

"What girl does he write letters to?" asked Maykanova.

"I don't know…He wrote on top just the letter 'Zh' and below added, 'Let's be like Kozy Korpesh and Bayan-slu.'"

I came to my senses somehow and fired off:

"That's not true!"

"It's true, it's true! I saw how you wrote this several days ago, hiding the paper under the desk.

"That's not true!"

At first I really was scared that this scoundrel really could have grabbed one of my letters to Zhanar. Realizing that that hadn't happened, I caught my breath in relief and pulled myself together. I stole a glance at Zhanar, but I couldn't see her face. She sat with her eyes lowered, her head in her hands.

Fortunately, no one paid particular attention to the talk about the letter. Most likely they decided that this was the usual gossip from the blabbermouth Zhantas.

"Does anyone else have anything to say?" once again Maykanova asked.

There were no others who wished to talk.

Finally, the proposals of the students were put to a vote.

"Who is for not expelling Kadyrov from school and declaring a strict reprimand to him?"

The overwhelming majority were for this.

"Who is for expelling Kadyrov from school?"

One hand was raised in the classroom. It was Zhantas' hand.

CHAPTER TWENTY-SIX

Which Will Lead us To Chapter Twenty-Seven

A tumultuous, stormy sea. Mixing sky and water, a strong hurricane rages above. A lone boatman, which landed in the storm, tries to hold his own in an unequal battle with the playful elements. The white-crested waves standing on end toss the fragile boat like a wood chip up to the sky and then fiercely toss it below almost to the bottom. The unfortunate boatman is utterly out of strength and has lost any hope for a rescue. He has nothing left to do but gaze with fright at the avalanche of water bearing down on him and await his fate…

This is how I mentally imagined what I went through in recent days. The hurricane finally passed, and I was safe. Now I could collect my thoughts, make sense of some things and come to some conclusions.

Of course, I was to blame for everything myself. It was, after all, my personal lack of discipline and bad character that had led me to these consequences. Could anything like this have happened if I had been restrained and set an example like our Temir? And would my poor Mama have to drop work at the *jaylyau* and hurry home to the aul at full speed? If I were obedient and calm, she wouldn't have so many trials and tribulations. That's it, enough! Time to stop these stupid pranks. I must reform.

I'll admit that I wasn't making a promise to myself for the first time. There had been many such promises – and they were all sincere. However, no matter how I tried to be quiet, nothing ever came of it. I myself didn't notice how somehow in the heat of emotion, or for some other reason, I would do the latest bad deed. But now this couldn't happen again!

In the morning, Mama got ready to go back to the *jaylyau*. I led the horse in and saddled it. Mama came up to me and stroked my head and said:

"Well, Kozhatay, you're a smart boy after all and you should understand everything. If you do one more bad thing, don't be offended at me. I've had enough of these torments. I can't suffer to the end of my days for your bad deeds. I will leave you this house and everything that your father left and I myself will go away."

With these words, a vision of Karatay came up before my eyes, together with his beat-up old motorcycle. He was chuckling into his mustache and looking at me triumphantly as if to say: yes, I will take your mother away, and you will be left with your azhe to keep house in this home.

I hurled myself at Mama and threw my arms around her.

"No, don't leave, Mamochka, don't go, please! Let me sink through the ground here if I ever hurt you!" my voice shook and tears sprang to my eyes.

Mama placed an arm on my shoulder.

"If you will behave yourself, I will never leave."

"Don't get married, Mamochka…"

"What do I need a husband for? For me there is no greater happiness than raising you to be a man," Mama replied.

Soon she left for the *jaylyau* and I headed off to school. My mood was uplifted and cheerful. Mama's words still rang in my ears "What would I need a husband for? For me there is no greater happiness than raising you to be a man." Trust me, Mamochka! I will become a man, I will definitely become a man! You'll see what a wonderful writer I will become! Now I'm not like I was yesterday, but a different Kozha. A changed Kozha. And today is the first day of my new life!

In front of the home of Grandmother Nuripa, I saw a black dog which was hungrily gnawing at a bone. I stealthily picked up a small stone from the ground and was about to come closer to throw it at the dog. Suddenly, I was struck by a thought. "*Yapyray*, what has that dog ever done to me? Why should I hit it? And the owner will likely come running out of the house due to the noise and will start swearing and threatening me. And there would be yet another hooligan's act!" I thought.

I threw the stone away in the bushes and mentally cursing myself, went along the road. Around the turn, on the next street, I saw Zhanar, walking ahead. Her brown uniform dress fitter her small and slender figure beautifully. Zhanar had on her head my favorite red beret.

Wings sprouted unexpectedly from my back. I hurried ahead and quickly caught up with her. Hearing hurried steps behind her, Zhanar turned around.

"Hello, Zhanar."

"Hello!"

My glance felt to a small white spot on Zhanar's left shoulder.

"You've got a spot on your shoulder," I said.

She stopped and turned her head.

"Where"?

"Here," I easily wiped off the spot with my fingers, which disappeared. But I continued to rub it, unable to take my hand off her shoulder.

"Thanks," said Zhanar.

We walked along side by side.

107

"You were probably really scared that they were going to kick you out of school?" she asked me.

"So you say! What do I have to be afraid of? If they had kicked me out, I would have gone to my *nagashi* in Sartogai and would keep studying. Do you know what kind of school they have there?

"What kind?"

"It's two stories! And if you could see the gym they have at that school..."

I realized that I was spouting nonsense and shut up. A minute later, I suddenly fired off:

"Zhanar!"

"What?"

"Do you want to know who I wrote the letter to?"

"What letter?"

"Well, the letter that Zhantas talked about in the meeting."

Zhanar's face turned red.

"Who did you write it to?"

But now I was tongue-tied.

"I was just kidding," I barely managed to mutter.

CHAPTER TWENTY SEVEN

In Which the Secret Meeting Will Be Described, With That My Tale Will End

After dinner, I went to the far room to turn on the table lamp and pull the curtains tight on the window, so that no one could see anything. There was a mirror in the corner of the room. I moved the table up close to it, and sat down to face this violator of public order, famous for his pranks throughout the whole district, Kozha.

"I declare the secret meeting of one person – Kadyrov Kozha – to be open. On the agenda there is only one question: what should I do in the future in order to become a disciplined and exemplary student?"

I earnestly wrote down the agenda in the minutes of the meeting and looked at the disturber of the peace.

"Well, go ahead and talk, *batyr*[64]!"

It seemed as if the shameless fellow was taking all of this as a joke, because his smiling mug looked back at me. Worse, he was squinting his eyes, sticking out his lip, twisting his mouth and clearly mocking me. This really made me mad! I knit my brows ominously, and imitating Akhmetov, banged my fist on the desk.

"Stand!"

The "*batyr*" obediently jumped up in fright.

"Sit!"

He sat down in his seat just as obediently.

"Why have you called me, Kozhatay?" azhe asked, coming into the room.

"I didn't call you, go back to your room."

"I thought I heard your voice?"

"I'm not talking to you, it's nothing. There's a secret meeting in session, don't bother me."

"What's a session?" said *azhe*, not understanding.

---

[64] A *batyr* is a warrior.

"What, you don't know what a session is? Well, in general, there's a meeting underway, do you understand? A meeting!"

Azhe froze for a moment in surprise and then looked at me in fear.

"Lord, what are you talking about? What meeting? Why have you put the table up to the mirror?"

"Go on," I said in frustration. "What business is it of yours? I'll explain one more time: I'm holding a secret meeting and I am discussing my personal case, do you understand? You can't be at it!"

Azhe came closer to me. Her wide, reddened and watery brown eyes stared at me intently.

"Kozhatay, my dear, say: '*bismillah*[65]!' Well, say it my dear, 'bismillah!' You talked in your sleep last night about some meeting and discussion, apparently, this is all from fright. Well, say: '*bismillah*!'"

I couldn't stand it any more and cried out three times in a row:

"Bismillah! Bismillah! Bismillah!" and then asked:

"Is that enough? Or do I need more?"

"My little sun, can a person really hold a meeting with himself? I think you probably read too much last night…Maybe you're not getting enough sleep?

I jumped up from my seat.

"*Azhe*, dear, go in your room, don't bother me, please!"

Somehow, I led the old lady who hesitantly kept standing in place through the door and hooked the lock.

…The secret meeting lasted about an hour. As a result, the following decree was drafted and unanimously passed:

"*FIRST:* An undisciplined person looks repulsive in people's eyes. I have finally been convinced of this. Furthermore, it is very harmful for his future. A person who cannot behave properly cannot be accepted into the *Komsomol*[66]. Accordingly, I must definitely become disciplined:

For this:

a) In the future I will not get into fights with anyone and will behave calmly. I will try to live in peace both with my friend and enemy.

WARNING! If anybody comes after me, I must warn him: "Go your way, or you will regret it!" If that does not work, and he keeps bothering me, then I consider it possible to put my fists into motion as a form of self-defense.

b) From this day forth, I promise not to pronounce a single bad or crude word. I will treat both older and younger people with respect.

SECOND: For each bad deed, I must immediately receive a ruthless punishment. The forms of punishment are as follows:

a) If I start fighting or get into a fight, then that day, I will have no supper.

---

[65] *Bismillah* is the first phrase of a Muslim prayer, "In the name of God".
[66] The *Komsomol* was the Communist Youth league in the Soviet Union.

b) If I call anybody undeservedly a bad word, then I will sit at home on Sunday and will not go even a step outside. In other words, I will put myself under house arrest.

c) If I get a reprimand from the teacher in class for bad behavior, then during the break I will sit at my desk and not go outside.

d) I had a habit of strictly punishing, beating or driving from the yard all alien chickens, geese, dogs, cats, lambs and goats that wondered into our yard. That was how I killed the red rooster of our neighbor Almas. This is not acceptable behavior. This can be done quietly and calmly. If such a thing repeats, I must run up to the upper chicken farm and back two times without a stop.

THIRD: My friendship with Sultan from this day forth is ended, and our oath from this day forth is not in force. As for the red hearth in the other world, I can say that I don't believe in god, and therefore the punishing fire doesn't scare me at all.

FOURTH: Good studying is the main sign of an exemplary student. In this quarter, I must become one of the best pupils in our class. In order to achieve this, I:

a) will not miss a single hour of lessons without a good excuse;

b) will do all my homework assignments carefully and on time;

FIFTH: In order for all these obligations taken above to be fulfilled unfailingly, every evening, before I go to bed, I will write in this notebook all my good and bad deeds.

Fulfillment of these terms is an enormous trial for me.

If I cannot successfully cope with them, then I shouldn't keep going to school. Then I will have to find some other path for myself in order to grow up a worthy man and not torment my poor mother needlessly.

Thus, the decree was unanimously passed.

Now behind the door there were some steps and voices heard. They were tugging and knocking on the door.

"Kozhatay, my little sun, open up!"

I got up, unhooked the lock and opened the door. Azhe and the old man Aybakir were standing there.

They looked at me strangely somehow, and cautiously.

"*Salamaleykum*, Grandfather."

"Hello, sonny. Why is it that if you are sitting alone in the room, you put the lock on?"

"Oh, I was just…studying my lessons."

"*Kozhatay*, my dear, let Grandfather feel your pulse," azhe said pleadingly.

I was frightened.

"Why? What happened?"

"You slept poorly last night and had bad dreams all night. Who knows…Let Grandfather listen to your pulse. And you don't look very well today."

I couldn't help but laugh.

"Oh, *azhe*! You are so dense! You think I am sick? I don't have any illnesses, I'm absolutely healthy." I gave azhe a loud kiss on her wrinkled forehead and ran out into the yard. What a great night it was! Beautiful! The moon shone brightly. It was a deep, cloudless sky, like a dark blue silk tent, casting its twinkling shimmer over the world. From the direction of the club there were sounds of an accordion, and the noisy voices of the guys. A living fire seemed to light in my chest, filling me with internal energy. I ran to the club. Before me in the dark sky hung the silvery sliver of moon, at the very edge of the aul was the mysteriously twinkling creek. How wonderful it was all around! It seemed as if nature was saying to me, "Fly ahead! Fly higher!" and was ready to give me powerful wings so that I could reach the heights of my highest dream. Burn! Burn brighter, fire of my soul! Fly higher, magical bird of my dream! I hurry and strive with impatience to you, tomorrow, awaiting me.

Moscow, 1956
Almaty, 1959